KU-072-938
Bolton Council
BROMLEY CROSS
01204 332354
IBL 16.4.15
BOLTON LIBRARIES
BT 144 0601 2

INTO THE TREES

by the same author

Luke and Jon
How the Trouble Started

Into the Trees

ROBERT WILLIAMS

ff

FABER & FABER

First published in 2014
by Faber & Faber Limited
Bloomsbury House
74–77 Great Russell Street, London WC1B 3DA
Typeset by Faber
Printed in England by CPI Group (UK) Ltd, Croydon, CR0 4YY

A CIP record for this book
is available from the British Library

ISBN 978-0-571-30817-0

2 4 6 8 10 9 7 5 3 1

For Mum and Dad and Heather

Abbeystead, 1990

They came through the trees on a Sunday evening. Four men in petrol-blue overalls, balaclavas covering their heads. They stepped out from the forest and onto the narrow road in front of them. The house they approached was a barn conversion in a secluded corner of Bleasdale Forest, a large detached building of thick stone and wood deep in the Abbeystead countryside. The men crossed the road, strode up the short drive and knocked on the door as politely as a visiting friend.

Harriet was lying on the floor reading a book, which was quickly boring her, when the knock came. She leapt up and ran to the door as if she was in a race: fists pumping, face determined, knees high. She was eight years old, it was a rare treat to have a visitor, and she was intent on getting there before anyone else. She dragged the door open with force. 'Hello,' she said, a little breathless, before looking up at the boiler suits and covered heads gathered in front of her. Harriet didn't know to scream. There was a second's pause before the man who'd knocked, the leader, took Harriet's hand and walked into the quiet house with her at his side. Harriet went easily, the other men followed.

'Who is it, love?' Thomas called over the top of his paper.

The group followed the sound of his voice.

Part One

One

Maltham, 1982

Like all babies Harriet Norton cried, but when Harriet cried it was different. It was a sound to make animals turn and run, a noise to terrify parents. And it would last for hours. Ann and Thomas Norton tried everything, but nothing calmed her, nothing soothed her, there was no special knack. They rocked, rubbed and massaged Harriet, they changed her whether or not she needed to be changed, fed her even if she'd just been fed, sang for her until they ran out of songs to sing. Thomas would put her in the car and drive out of town, up over hills, down into dark neighbouring valleys, even as far as one of the three big cities, hoping that the travel, the movement, would calm her. He was pulled over by the police once, in the bleak early hours, as he drove slowly, dozily, Harriet twisting and roaring behind him. He was quickly told to drive on when the noise hit the police officer, who slapped the roof of the car in sympathy as he turned away, thinking he'd forgotten how loud babies could cry, not missing his own nights of broken sleep one bit. Thomas tried the radio hoping the shipping forecast, the news, or middle-of-the-road middle-of-the-night music would hold the key, but nothing did.

The Nortons bought new washing powder, they changed Harriet's bedding and sheets, they tried different nappies, fed her new milk formula, washed her in a different brand of soap, and when that made no difference, washed her in water only. Still nothing worked. Their doctor showed little concern. Babies cry and Harriet was a healthy little girl with strong lungs, she said. After four months of suffering, when they were exhausted and tearful, hardly able to string a sentence together any more, they took Harriet to see a doctor at a different practice – a favour arranged by a receptionist friend. The friend explained the problem to the doctor before the Nortons' appointment.

'But you told him we're not anxious parents?' Ann asked the friend. 'You told him this isn't normal crying?'

Dr Standish examined Harriet, asking questions about feeding and sleeping patterns as he did. He smiled at her, held her up in the air and dropped her down to his face, smiled again and danced her in his lap. He passed a gurgling and happy Harriet back to Ann and the Nortons braced themselves for his diagnosis. He looked at the exhausted parents opposite him and spoke the words they were dreading to hear:

'Babies cry, it's the only a thing a doctor can be certain of. You have a healthy daughter.'

But they were prepared to fight their corner this time – they'd discussed a counterattack.

'Babies don't cry like this,' Ann said, sitting up in her chair, pushing herself forward, trying to sound calm and sane but feeling hectic and disturbed. 'Daniel didn't cry like this, he cried, but not like this. You've never heard crying like it. Something isn't right, I'm sure of it.' She sat back. 'And we can't go on like this.'

Thomas took his wife's hand in his own and spoke before the doctor had a chance to respond. 'Ann is right. The crying, it's like nothing we've heard before, and it goes on and on until it sounds like she's hurting herself.'

But Dr Standish was resolute. 'Every baby is different,' he said. 'Some babies cry for hours, some sleep through the night from the first few weeks. I'm sure this is upsetting, and maybe you were lucky with your first child, but be reassured that there is nothing wrong with your daughter. It's natural and normal for babies to cry.'

He smiled at the Nortons and they knew they were defeated. And they knew that Harriet's crying wasn't natural or normal, but in the bright surgery, in the middle of the morning, with Harriet silent and sweet-smelling, as perfect as an apple, it was impossible to make their case. They stood up and left without thanking the doctor, behaviour that would have seemed impossible to them only weeks before. They drove home feeling trapped and hopeless.

Two

Harriet's crying was usually worse at night, when she was under covers in her cot. If it started as soon as she was put down it was a bad sign, an indication that it would go on for hours. There would sometimes be a silence mid-marathon, for twenty short minutes, and this interlude initially gave the Nortons hope, but they quickly learnt to recognise it for what it was – a brief break before the noise kicked back in at the same ridiculous volume. The crying and sleeplessness affected every aspect of their lives. They were too tired to see friends and discouraged visitors. Thomas felt useless and ineffective at work and occasionally fell asleep at his desk. Ann worried that they were neglecting Daniel, their two-year-old, because they were so exhausted they had no energy for games and playing. When they communicated it was only to pass along essential information relating to the care of the children and the running of the house. Their next-door neighbours, a friendly couple with no children of their own, put their house on the market without mentioning it to the Nortons. When Ann finally did notice the sign in the adjoining garden, she knew they must be moving because of Harriet and the all-night wailing and briefly wondered if she should feel any guilt, but her exhaustion was so complete it was a thought that disappeared as soon as it entered her head.

After the visit to the out-of-town doctor, at Ann's insistence, Thomas began to spend a night every week at Redgate Guest House – a cheap bed-and-breakfast in a small town fifteen miles away. He was reluctant to leave Ann with the children, but he needed some sleep to be able to perform his job at the bank, and he relented. The guesthouse was a tired, worn-out place, overlooking the edge of an industrial estate, somewhere he was unlikely to bump into anyone he knew, unlikely to have to provide awkward explanations. The rooms were clean enough, and importantly, quiet. Thomas would arrive at seven thirty, be in bed by eight and sleep a deathly sleep until he was woken by the alarm clock at six thirty the next morning. He didn't stay for breakfast and would be back home before seven to help Ann with the children, after which he would shower and change and set off to work with a slightly clearer head.

At first Ann refused the guesthouse. Running away was the sign of a failed mother, surely, but after four months of suffering Harriet's dreadful all-night screaming, she surrendered and left for a Friday night, almost too tired to feel any guilt. These occasional nights afforded Thomas and Ann a shot of relief, but they didn't come close to making up for the endless sleeplessness they were both enduring at home. What neither Thomas or Ann confessed to each other was that Harriet, on terrible crying nights, when the partner was at the guesthouse, spent a couple of hours in her car seat in the cupboard under the stairs. There her screaming, whilst audible, wasn't murderous, and the left-alone parent wasn't scared of doing something they could never be forgiven for.

Eventually, in desperation, they took Harriet to a paediatrician at a private hospital.

'Everything you can think of please, every test there is for babies,' Ann said.

The results came back to confirm that Harriet was a perfect little girl, healthy in every way. After the specialist delivered Harriet's clean bill of health he looked at Thomas and Ann and prepared to speak. Don't say it, Ann pleaded silently. Please don't say it's our fault.

'Babies are very sensitive to mood, Mr and Mrs Norton,' the specialist said. 'They can sense stress and tension. They react to the atmosphere around them.'

He allowed time for his words to be absorbed before he continued.

'The best thing you can both do is to try and relax and enjoy your beautiful little girl.'

Ann had stopped listening after his first sentence. Her face was a twisted grip. She saw the road to insanity in front of her. She was a hundred grenades and if someone so much as caught her elbow it would trigger an explosion that would kill everyone in distance. Thomas felt utter defeat.

Three

Two weeks after the verdict from the specialist Thomas took Harriet out in the car at night. He'd spent the previous night fast asleep at the guesthouse and wanted Ann to have a couple of peaceful hours. It was an evening in the middle of July and the street was still layered with the smells of summer. It had been a hot day and even close to midnight the air was warm and only just starting to lose its weight and stickiness. Thomas buckled a screaming Harriet into her car seat and set off. He drove north out of the town, on one of the small roads, and headed for the country. After a few miles he passed through a village called Shipton and then a hamlet he didn't know the name of. He reached a junction where if he turned right he would eventually loop back in the direction of Maltham and home. Harriet showed no sign of easing up, so instead he turned left and drove six miles to the summit of Liverstock Fell. He stopped the car at the top of the climb and looked down onto the valley below him. It was a deep gathering of darkness and shadow. He could just make out the fells marking the far side of the valley, low-slung smudges edging into the sky, and four miles below him, in the northwest corner of the valley, a fist of lights, a village tucked away down there. He considered turning back and heading for home, he'd come further than he'd intended and tiredness had crept up on him again, but Harriet let out a brutal and sustained scream, so Thomas eased the car into gear and began the descent into the Trough of Abbeystead.

He was only twelve miles from Maltham but already on the kind of unknown roads that didn't get many travellers at any time of year. He'd avoided these roads and this area all winter, his arms steering him away from tight rural roads, too remote to be gritted, but since spring he'd been heading this way more often, and sometimes, despite his tiredness and Harriet's crying, he enjoyed himself. He discovered that you could drive for miles on these country roads, hardly ever take the same route, and within twenty minutes of leaving Liverstock Fell you would be on the top of the hills at the opposite side of the valley, looking down onto the next valley in the chain. And sometimes, occasionally, Harriet would stop crying for a few minutes and Thomas, driving along ancient roads, past thick-bricked farmhouses and endless fields, in complete exhaustion, would feel serene.

Ann and Thomas hadn't spoken about Harriet's crying since the visit to the specialist. If there really was nothing wrong with her, no cause for her searing howling, then there was no cure to be found and nothing they could do. The only thing they'd learnt, at the cost of all that money, was their reaction to the crying could be making it worse. The unspoken hope was that as Harriet grew older, surely it would stop. A child can't cry forever, Thomas reasoned. He was wondering if they could survive another eighteen months when he turned onto a small lane that appeared at his left, a road he hadn't noticed before. The road twisted tightly between low trees and thick bushes for a couple of miles before it opened up and ran straight. Thomas relaxed, took his eyes from the road and looked up. He saw what appeared to be a huge black patch sewn into the horizon, but as he drove closer he could see it was a forest ahead of him, dark and densely packed. At that moment Thomas could think of nothing more thrilling than driving into a black forest in the middle of the night. The road led straight to the trees and although it widened as he entered the forest, the trees edged in on either side and the opposite felt true; Thomas increased his grip on the steering wheel. After following the road for five minutes Thomas saw a creature ahead, stood in the centre of the road. He slowed the car to a stop and peered into the dark. It was a deer, staring back at him. After a few seconds she turned her head away, stalked into the trees with robotic grace and was gone. It was then Thomas noticed the silence. He turned to check on Harriet. She was awake, looking back at him with wide-open eyes. Thomas knew she'd been screaming when he dropped down into the trough, and as they twisted along the tiny road, but he couldn't remember when it had stopped. He became aware of the smell then. The window was open and the rich scent of trees was strong in the air. Thomas steered the car to the side of the road and climbed out. He looked around him. The deer, the silence and the smell of the forest combined to wake him up. Here he was in the middle of the night, tiny under these huge trees, with his beautiful little girl. For the first time since he'd held Harriet in the minutes after she was born, happiness shocked him. He unbuckled Harriet, pulled her to his chest and carried her into the trees. He walked for twenty silent, happy minutes before fatigue struck and Thomas realised he was deep in a forest in the middle of the night, fifteen miles from home, his baby daughter warm and heavy in his arms. He found his way back to the car and set off for home, dreading how tired he would feel at work the next day.

Three nights later Thomas headed to the Trough of Abbeystead again, Harriet buckled in behind him. Harriet maintained her crying from cot to car and showed no sign of easing up during the journey. After three wrong turns he eventually found the road that crept under the low trees and then to the forest. Thomas opened the windows fully and drove towards the army of trees on the horizon. Then he was out of the car and walking, clutching Harriet close, and within five minutes she was quiet. It could be the smell of the trees, he thought, as he watched the ground, making sure his feet didn't catch on any roots. He walked for half an hour before sitting down against a tree trunk to rest. Harriet fell asleep quickly and after ten minutes Thomas rose and began the walk back to the car. Harriet remained silent throughout. In the car he sat for another few minutes with Harriet in his arms, flanked by giant trees, both of them quiet.

When a sleep-kick jerked Thomas awake he put Harriet in her seat, turned the car around and headed for home.

Thomas made the trip once more with the same results. As he drove back home that night he wondered what he could possibly say to Ann, but he decided not to explain, it would only sound ridiculous, and he planned to show her instead. He arranged for Ann's parents to have Daniel for the night and made sure that Ann spent the previous night at the guest-house, so she would be less exhausted and more likely to embark on the trip with him. He was nervous when he broached the subject.

'I think I may have found something which stops Harriet's crying,' he said, 'but if I explained it to you, you would think I was mad, so I want to show you instead. It will take a couple of hours, that's all.'

'I'll try anything,' Ann said.

Harriet was fed, washed and changed and put down at the usual time. Five minutes later the wailing began. Ann and Thomas tried all the tricks they knew wouldn't work and then left her upstairs, a tiny, livid ball of flesh, screaming at the ceiling. At eleven Thomas carried her to the car and they set off.

Thomas hadn't said a word to Ann about the destination; it seemed too silly to say out loud, and as they drove he worried that maybe he'd imagined the previous silences, that perhaps he'd been so tired his ears had shut down and the silent wanderings through the trees hadn't been silent at all, and he'd been a sleep-deprived man carrying a bellowing baby through a forest. Twenty-five minutes after leaving the house they turned on to the forest road, and it was then, with the sight of the distant trees in front of him, that the last drop of belief Thomas held deserted him. Harriet was behind him, screaming relentlessly, Ann was next to her, tense and exhausted, and Thomas wondered what he was doing. He slowed the car for the last mile as he approached the forest, to give Harriet time to settle, but she battled on regardless. They entered under the line of trees and Thomas drove on for a few minutes before pulling to a stop. He looked to Ann, put his hand on the car door and, without any confidence, said, 'Let's see.'

Thomas, Harriet and Ann walked into the trees.

Harriet fell quiet.

They walked for ten minutes, neither of them saying a word and then Thomas stopped, turned to Ann and said, 'This is the fourth time now.'

Ann took Harriet from Thomas and sat down,

Thomas crouched opposite. They stayed there for an hour before heading back to the car. The next night Thomas stayed at home with Daniel while Ann drove Harriet to the forest. She returned an hour later, hugged her husband in bed, and whispered, 'It works.'

Harriet screamed away in the next room.

They'd never camped before so Thomas went shopping and bought a tent and sleeping bags and anything else he could think of that they might need. On the Saturday night Thomas, Ann, Daniel and Harriet set off for Bleasdale Forest with a loaded car.

'Are we allowed to do this?' Ann asked, as they crested Liverstock Fell. 'Don't we need a permit or aren't we supposed to ask someone?'

Thomas shrugged, he'd briefly wondered himself, but was too tired to make any enquiries. He drove as far into the forest as he could, ending up on a tiny road that turned into nothing more than a track, and parked against a collapsing stone wall. They unpacked their gear and set off into the trees, quickly finding a spot for the tent. By nine everything was set up, Thomas and Ann were drinking tea from a flask and eating sandwiches, Daniel and Harriet were already asleep. Thomas and Ann were quick to follow the children and shortly the whole family was asleep. Harriet grumbled and moaned at times, and at four in the morning she cried for ten minutes, but Ann fed her and comforted her and she soon settled. Daniel didn't stir. They hadn't had a night as peaceful since before Harriet was born. At seven in the morning they took down the tent, packed everything away and walked back to the car. They were all quiet on the drive back, Harriet fell asleep and didn't cry, even when they left the forest behind. Ann began to laugh as they passed through Shipton and between gear changes she held hands with Thomas. They were back home by eight. That night, sat in the front room, Harriet screaming above them, Ann turned to Thomas and said:

'So what are we supposed to do?'

Four

Raymond Farren first saw Thomas and Harriet Norton on their second visit to Bleasdale Forest. They appeared in front of him in the early hours, and despite his shock at seeing someone else in the forest in the middle of the night, he managed to manoeuvre his clumsy body behind a tree unnoticed and hold his breath until they passed. He was a big, square man with a large face, thick lips and heavy hands. When he walked it was with a clumsy stiffness – as though he was dragging himself along by his neck, a broken machine of a man. He was working for a farmer called Chapman, sleeping in a caravan on his land. Despite the physical nature of the work Raymond often found it impossible to sleep, and walked in the forest at night to pass the time and encourage tiredness. He only worked for Chapman when he was needed, the rest of the time he was at home in Etherton, in his small terraced house, with nothing to do, so he did his sleeping then, spending days under the covers. Raymond believed his body stored up energy during those unhappy weeks and was so rested by the time he was required to work, it refused to acknowledge the night and allow him any sleep. On the nights it felt as if tiredness would never visit again Raymond left his caravan and walked, and because he didn't want to be known as the mad night-walker, because he didn't want the people of Abbeystead gossiping about him any more than they might already do, he crossed the road and headed into the trees, into Bleasdale Forest, where there was no fear of being spotted. Under cover he walked until weariness eventually began to affect him, when he would return to the caravan with the prospect of a short sleep in the early hours. In the years he'd been night-walking in the forest he'd never seen another soul. Even the forest animals were shy, and given plenty of warning by his crashing size fifteen feet. When he came across Thomas and Harriet Norton he was as shocked as if he'd stumbled on a city amongst the trees. He was in the western side of the forest when he heard a sharp cough ahead of him. He looked up and saw a man heading towards him, a bundle at his front. Within seconds the man passed a hidden Raymond, and Raymond could see that the bundle was a baby. He also saw a defeated, exhausted look on the man's face and Raymond was filled with a cold fear.

It was a cloudless summer evening, even under the thick canopy of the forest it wasn't black, and the man was walking slowly, wearily, so Raymond didn't need to be too close to follow. He stalked as stealthily as his awkward body allowed. Eventually the man stopped and rested against a tree. Raymond tensed, but the man's arms made no movement; they remained gently around the baby at his front. After a few minutes he stood up and headed back the way he'd come. Raymond followed him to Rabbit Lane and a car, and watched from the trees. The man climbed into the car, tipped his head back and closed his eyes. The trough has been used for this kind of thing before, thought Raymond. They come here because it's remote, so they won't be stopped or found by the wrong people when they've done what they came to do. The man could do what he liked to himself, Raymond saw no sin in that, but he couldn't let anything happen to the baby. As soon as the hosepipe was brought from the boot he would step out from the trees. During those minutes, watching, braced, Raymond was alive. More alive than when his mother had finally succumbed to the barrage of illnesses that had attacked her at the end of her life, more alert than the first time he rested at the top of Marshaw Fell and looked out on the view of Abbeystead below him.

The man closed his eyes.

'He's thinking about it,' Raymond whispered under his breath. 'He's rallying himself.'

Suddenly the man jerked forward, his eyes sprang open, he looked confused, and then his shoulders dropped. He kissed the small head in his arms, strapped the baby into a car seat and drove away quickly. Raymond walked back to the caravan, knowing sleep wouldn't come at all that night. He would feel the last of the adrenaline twitching its way through his body as he led the cows for milking at half past five in the morning, still wondering what he'd been witness to.

Five

Thomas spent the weekends walking and driving the roads in and around Bleasdale Forest. It was a huge place, miles wide and deep, and many times he found himself lost. On his wanderings he came across houses, tucked away up a lane, hidden in a sudden dell, but none of them displayed sale signs, and no local estate agents knew of any properties available within the forest boundaries.

'We'll put you on a list,' he was told, but Thomas shook his head at that. He didn't have time to sit on a list.

Instead of staying at the guesthouse midweek, Thomas would spend a night camping in the forest, and on Saturday nights the whole family packed up and headed to the trees with their tent and sleeping bags. Harriet did cry on these nights, but it was the crying they'd been used to when Daniel was a baby, crying that could be soothed away, or would eventually end of its own accord. Ann, who'd never been camping before these last few weeks, found herself longing for the Saturday nights in the trees, where she would finally be afforded a few hours of deep sleep.

The Nortons were at a loss. Sat in their front room in Maltham, lying in a tent underneath the trees, the conversation varied little.

'What is it about the forest?'

'The trees? The smell? Maybe it calms her, soothes her.'

'I know, but every time? It works every time. She screams the house down every day and as soon as we take her to the forest she's silent. How?'

'I've no idea.'

'You don't think we're imagining it, do you? You don't think we've lost it?'

'It had crossed my mind, but both of us imagining the same thing?'

They began to experiment. They walked Harriet through a local wood, they bought pine air freshener for her bedroom, they bought two small indoor trees and put them on either side of Harriet's cot. None of it worked.

Thomas found the barn on one of his walks. It was in the southeast corner of the forest, set back from a small road, which dipped, rose and twisted through the trees. The barn was almost a ruin. There was a huge gaping hole where the door would have been and only half a roof. It was a big space, tall and deep. In one corner stood a rusty tractor with flat tyres, old oil cans were thrown together against the back wall and a washing machine sat abandoned in the middle of it all, somehow still white, vulnerable in the dirt. The barn was a wreck. But it was surrounded by trees. Without allowing himself to think too much about what he was doing Thomas walked further along the road, heading for the nearest house, looking for somewhere he could ask questions.

Back at home that night Thomas waited until Daniel and Harriet were in bed before he said anything.

'And she would be prepared to sell it?' Ann asked.

'She didn't seem against it. But it's a shell; it would need a lot of work. We would have to strip it down and start again.'

'Why would we want to buy a shell?'

'We can't wait for a house to come on the market, and it's unlikely we would get planning permission for a new building out there, but because there is already a structure standing, just about standing, we can ask for permission to renovate it.'

'How much does she want?'

'It wasn't discussed. I think she would probably want to meet us before she decided to sell. The cost would be in the building work though.'

Ann looked at the wine in her glass.

'What did you say? You just walked up, knocked on her door and asked if you could buy her barn?'

'Pretty much. I explained that we lived in Maltham, that we loved the area and it was just what we had been looking for.'

'And she said "OK"?'

'Not exactly. She was worried it would be too dark, with all the trees, so I explained we loved trees. That we are a tree family.'

'We're certainly that,' Ann said, and put her glass down. 'So what do we do next?'

'We see what happens with Harriet. There's no point in doing anything if Harriet isn't happy with it.'

The next evening Thomas drove Harriet to Bleasdale Forest and the barn. He took her from the car and walked through the gaping wall and over to the washing machine. Harriet wriggled in his arms but made no sound. Thomas rested against the washing machine and within minutes Harriet was asleep. They stayed there for an hour. Thomas took Harriet to the barn several times over the next week, each time with the same result, and so, on the next Saturday afternoon, the four of them went to see Mrs Silverwood. During the drive Thomas tried not to think about what he was attempting, it seemed ridiculous when he considered it in any detail, so he chatted with Ann and kept his thoughts away from the reason for the visit.

It was a quiet afternoon for Harriet, she was in the forest, and Daniel was on adorable form, smiling at Mrs Silverwood, chatting away in gobbledegook. It seemed to Thomas that nobody wanted to broach the subject of the barn. They spoke about Thomas's job at the bank, if Ann would go back to work when the children were older. Mrs Silverwood told them about her children, now moved away, about her dead husband, Harry. How he'd been born in the house they were sitting in, and had lived and farmed in Abbeystead all his life. It wasn't until everyone had finished their drinks and eaten the biscuits from the offered plate that the barn was mentioned.

'Do you really want to buy it? That wreck?' Mrs Silverwood asked.

'We do,' Thomas said, and Ann nodded.

'It can be lonely out here,' Mrs Silverwood warned,

'and the winters can be hard. Cold and long.' She turned to Daniel. 'What about you, Daniel?' she asked. 'What do you think?'

'Biscuit!' he shouted, and Mrs Silverwood laughed.

Thomas leant forward with his arms resting on his knees. 'But we don't want to cause you trouble,' he said. 'We don't want to inconvenience you. You're not that near the barn, but there will be lots of work going on, traffic coming and going on that small road when the work is being done.'

He was thinking – I don't mean that at all, I don't care if it causes you a world of trouble. I want that barn for my family.

Mrs Silverwood wasn't concerned. 'As long as you are sure it's what you want,' she said. She went to make more drinks and brought out another plate of biscuits.

Thomas set to it. He was imbued with an energy he'd never known before, a desire to get things done. He was ready for the battle and became single-minded in his aim. He found an architect and paid him extra to draw up plans as quickly as possible. He delivered the plans to the planning department and hounded them until they grew sick of him. In record time, although it felt an age to Thomas, the plans were approved. He didn't allow himself a second's celebration, instead he phoned builders and negotiated and haggled and checked what they said with other tradesmen and pulled them up when he thought they were trying it on. He made a receptionist at the solicitor's cry when he thought she was stalling him. He felt remorse only for a second before his brain moved on to the next thing that needed to be done. When timescales were suggested he cut them in half, saying he was sure it could be done more quickly, and he found that he was right – in most cases the work could be done more quickly, if he was willing to pay. He started each morning with a list and enjoyed pushing a thick black line through each task as he pushed his family, as quickly, as strongly as he could, closer to a new home in the trees.

Selling their house was easy. It was a good house in a good town with popular schools close by. They had four offers and accepted the one from the couple with no chain. It wasn't the most money, but the buyer was prepared to wait until the Nortons had a house they could move into. The visit to Ann's parents to ask for money had been awkward. The Steads had the money and would give anything to see Ann and their grandchildren happy, but they couldn't understand the move at all.

'You already have such a lovely home. You were so happy to find it and you've spent so much money on it,' Judith said.

'And why out there?' George asked. 'What will you do, day in day out?'

Ann and Thomas did their best to sell the idea. They spoke about the countryside, the fresh air, the nature, the kids being able to explore without fear, but Ann's parents remained nonplussed. The money was not withheld however and Thomas and Ann thanked them sincerely for it.

'We could just tell them the real reason, you know,' Thomas said. 'They know we've had problems with Harriet.'

'I would happily tell them the truth if it didn't sound so insane,' Ann said, and Thomas nodded. The fact that it was a simple truth didn't make it sound any less absurd when you spoke it out loud. They were renovating a wrecked barn, in the middle of a remote forest, because it was the only place they'd found that their baby daughter didn't cry.

Six

Raymond was considered an oddball in Abbeystead not only because of his size and appearance, but because he was never seen in any of the local pubs, didn't socialise at all, and on the rare occasions he was spotted in the village, avoided eye contact and didn't nod or offer a greeting to anyone. Frank Chapman, the farmer who employed him, would sometimes be questioned about Raymond at the bar of the Tillotsons in Keasden. A terse man himself, he would say, 'He works hard and doesn't say much.'

Sheila Chapman would offer a little more when she accompanied her husband on a weekend night. 'He's a good man, he's just not good with other people. He's not sure what to do around them, he's very shy. We've never had any problems with him at all. And he's a good worker, isn't he Frank?'

Frank would nod at that, and think, cheap too. He sometimes worried that Raymond would be offered more money for less work elsewhere, but whenever summoned, Raymond would turn up, bag over his shoulder, and always within twenty-four hours.

Raymond needed the meagre wages, but he didn't work at the farm just for money. He had to escape his house. Home was a rundown terraced house in Etherton, a damp mess he'd inherited from his mother. The damp patches had first seeped in through the downstairs front room, but over the years they'd spread, along with the black mould. In the small back bedroom, which had been Raymond's as a child, the mould ran from the bottom of the wall, up to the ceiling and across to the door, like a colony of escaping wasps. Raymond kept the door shut on that room and only went in if he had to. Wallpaper flaked off the walls in the downstairs rooms, the brick underneath crumbling a little too. For a couple of years Raymond repapered when the wallpaper hung loose, but within weeks, sometimes days, the paper would curl away from the wall again, as if in disgust, and Raymond could sense the dampness pouring through and his pulse would quicken. The house was dying. With him inside. The place smelt dank, an odour of old vegetables clung to the air. It was a greasy smell which embedded itself into the fabric of Raymond's clothes, worked into the pores of his skin and was so familiar to Raymond he didn't notice it when he was living at the house, was surprised by its pungency when he returned after a few weeks on the farm. The smells of the farm, even at their most ripe, smelt of life, whilst 11 Granville Road smelt of death and nothing else. Raymond would have gladly swapped the house permanently for the old caravan behind the farmhouse of a farmer who paid him too little and didn't seem to like him very much at all.

Raymond loved to escape his house. He loved to escape Etherton. He once heard the town described as 'an armpit of a town', a description which summed up his feelings with precision. There were streets of abandoned houses, blocks of flats built only twenty years before and already condemned, empty, crumbling mills on the fringes of the town, high, dark hills behind them. In winter the hills trapped the rain and mist, leaving the town to wallow for months in a damp bowl of cold moisture, Raymond's house a sponge in the middle, sucking it all in, swallowing it down. In summer the hills funnelled the sun's beams firmly, refusing entry to any cross-blowing winds, and the town cooked like an egg on a scalding pavement.

Abbeystead was Raymond's haven. Fifteen miles

away – a million miles in his head. Even on a black winter's day, the landscape ugly and raw, rebuilding a stone wall in a high field when none of the stones were the right stones and his fingers were so cold it hurt to touch anything, he didn't want to be anywhere else. He sometimes imagined a police car turning up at his caravan in the middle of the night to take him away, his crime to believe a man like him would be allowed to spend time in a place like Abbeystead.

Raymond had been working the farms in Abbeystead for years, from the age of seventeen. After school had finished he'd visited the job centre and found work as a labourer, but Raymond wasn't good in large groups, and on the sites there were so many men, their numbers and faces changed daily, and it was hard to keep up. Some of the men meant what they said, others said the opposite of what they meant. It exhausted Raymond. But what he disliked most was working in Etherton. Converting mills into flats, converting mills into community centres, quite often stripping mills bare before they were pulled down. He felt like he was forever trapped in the back streets of an armpit of a town he'd grown to hate. Eventually he plucked up courage, returned to the job centre and asked if there was anything else going.

The man behind the desk looked Raymond over, noticed his huge hands, shuffled some cards and said, 'What about farming?'

Raymond thought of green fields, leaping lambs, and nodded. He held his hand out for the card.

'They don't advertise,' the man said. 'Most of them can't write. You'll have to go out there and chance it. And the money won't be as good as it is on the sites. They're a tight bunch, farmers.'

Less money didn't concern Raymond too much, but he couldn't turn up at a stranger's door and ask for work, it was an impossible thing for him to do. He left the job centre resigned to more labouring. But after a terrible day on a new site, a site he was contracted to work for weeks, Raymond got on his bike and rode the fifteen miles to Abbeystead with the intention of pushing himself over the mountain of his shyness. He loved the place the first time he looked down from the top of Marshaw Fell. He wondered why nobody had told him it existed. Here it was, all in front of him, a bike ride away from his dark town. Abbeystead stretched out below him: forests, rivers, fields, and so much space, everything unfolding to its full size, no tight streets, no buildings crammed together, jimmied up against one another. Knocking at the first door was the hardest thing Raymond had ever done, but also the most rewarding. He'd chanced on the Roeburn farm, and although they didn't need anyone, they sent him to someone who did, and on the same morning Raymond landed his first farming job. Word spread that he was strong and worked hard and at certain times of the year, for a few years, he could pick and choose which jobs on what farms. But suddenly, it seemed, the farms grew smaller, some disappeared altogether and Raymond went from juggling jobs for different farmers to relying on the hours Chapman could offer and the small wages he paid. But Raymond wasn't an expectant man and it was enough. To be out of Etherton, working in Abbeystead, was enough.

Seven

In only six months the Nortons moved in. They were living in a shell, everything to be completed, but the roof, the windows, the walls and the floors were in place. They had electricity, they had heating.

The first night was terrifying.

After all the work had been done, the negotiation, the haggling, the hassling, the worry and stress of it, and all of it dealt with on hardly any sleep, they were scared to see if it had been for nothing. Eventually Harriet fell asleep in the lounge downstairs and Thomas carried her up to her room. He lowered her, as gently as he could, as if he was handling sleep itself, into her cot and she wriggled and moaned, but Thomas held his breath and she quietened. Thomas couldn't leave the room, he didn't dare. He sat in the corner and willed the silence to continue. Ann stayed downstairs, sitting forward in her chair, listening, waiting, for the crying to start, her back as hard as the bare concrete floor under her feet. After twenty minutes she crept upstairs and sat down with Thomas, resting her head against his arm, where she fell asleep. Harriet slept through. On the third silent night Ann cried. On the fourth night Ann and Thomas made love.

Eight

Raymond watched the transformation take place. On a midnight walk he stepped out of the trees to see an old tractor, a washing machine and other junk lined up in front of the ruined barn. A couple of nights later they were gone, replaced with piles of bricks, slates and timber. Thick tyre tracks seared into the grass at the edge of the forest, the thin road barely able to contain the vehicles that had been visiting. Something was happening. It pleased Raymond to have a destination to visit on his walks, it gave a direction and reason to his wandering, and he maintained a keen eye on the barn. Progress was quick. Within weeks walls were rebuilt and the new roof was in place. Chapman didn't need him for a month-long period and when the call finally came and he returned to the farm, Raymond was keen to see how much further work had been done. When he stepped out of the trees on his first night back, it was a house stood in front of him. There was still no front door so Raymond walked through the building one last time. He went up the stairs and into the bedrooms and tried to imagine how it would look when it was finished. Raymond couldn't help feeling envious; this was a house he would have given anything to own, hidden in the heart of Abbeystead, underneath the trees. A beautiful building, out of sight. The perfect house.

Raymond ate his meals in the kitchen of the farmhouse with Frank and Sheila Chapman and it was there, a week later, he learnt about the Nortons.

'It's a family from Maltham with two young kids,' Sheila said. 'One day they knocked on the door and asked old Silverwood if it was for sale and she sold them it.'

'I bet she did,' Chapman said. 'And I bet she got a price for it.'

Sheila nodded her agreement and stood up to clear the table. Raymond rose to help.

'But if they think it's going to be easy up here, if they think it's going to be sunsets and country fairs, they'll be in for a shock,' she said. Raymond passed her the plates and she scraped chicken skin and cold gravy dregs into a bucket. 'They will be in for a shock,' she repeated. Chapman stayed at the table, lit a cigarette and said, 'I bet she did get a price for it.'

It pleased Raymond that there would be a family in the barn. He couldn't understand why more people didn't buy barns and turn them into houses in the countryside. Not too many of course, then it would just be like the towns, but there was enough space in Abbeystead, enough broken old barns for a few more to come. When he heard about the amount of money houses sold for in cities it made Raymond dizzy. Why! Why spend all that money on a house amongst thousands of other houses, with noisy, nosey neighbours, and crowds of people everywhere? Why do that when you could live here? Raymond didn't understand how people's brains worked.

Nine

Mornings in Abbeystead were as close to heaven as Thomas Norton thought it was possible to be. He would drink a cup of tea at the kitchen table in the quiet hour before the family woke and silence was sent scurrying into the corners. He would wash and dry the cup and leave the house at half past six for his walk. He varied the route depending on the weather, the time of year and his mood. Sometimes he walked through the trees, sometimes he climbed Lowgill Fell, occasionally he walked a shorter walk to Mrs Silverwood's house and back. Like Raymond Farren, Thomas couldn't quite believe that Abbeystead was there for him, for free, every day. The mornings, as Abbeystead gathered itself to life, were wonderful to Thomas, and he took his time on these walks, tried to spot the changes to the trees and plants throughout the year. He felt ashamed that he could hardly name any of the flowers that grew alongside the road, he wasn't even sure about the different species of trees he passed under, so he bought a book to teach himself. But it wasn't easy – he'd study a tree, flick through the book to find the corresponding picture and would see that the tree could be one of several, or sometimes there would be no picture that resembled the tree in front of him at all. He grew frustrated with his lack of progress and stopped taking the book out with him. But he still found the early morning walks helped sustain him through his day at work, where he would have to deal with colleagues and customers and their moods and emotions. Thomas didn't enjoy his job and throughout his working day he held on to the thought that at half past five he would be driving out of the town, on the quiet roads, up onto the hills and minutes later he would be dropping down into Abbeystead, heading to his home and family in the forest. And best of all, he still had the night to come. He liked to watch as the trough shaded, slowly at first, before night finally and suddenly took hold, dropping a blanket of black entirely over everything. The moment it happened thrilled Thomas. It was absolute, medieval. In summer he would sit on a plastic garden chair at the back of the house with a glass of beer, watch the sky darken and the trees back away into the night. A shiver would run through him. His children were in bed asleep, his wife was curled up on the settee, he was guarding his frontier.

Ann was less happy. The new lease of life that struck Thomas refused to attach itself to her. It was months after the move before she noticed the grumbling dissatisfaction. At first Ann was exhausted and catching up on sleep was blissful, that was enough for a while. And then they'd begun to finish and furnish the house and that had absorbed her. When it was finally done she could see that the house looked good, that it was a house to be proud of, a house to be envious of even. She sat back and patiently waited for the converted barn to start feeling like a home. But despite the fact she'd chosen the carpets, the curtains, decided on the colour of the walls, hung the paintings herself, the house refused to yield, refused to welcome her. Ann thought that perhaps it was because nobody had lived there before; there were no memories buried in the walls, no notes hidden under the floorboards. Maybe a house has to earn its homeliness, she decided; maybe you can't just throw up bricks and a roof, put down some carpet and expect a place to feel like home immediately. So she waited, but the change didn't come. She suspected it wasn't just the house, that the location played a part in her unease, and it struck her why one afternoon as she read a book on the settee, the rain crashing onto their new roof, gurgling into the new gutters – it felt like she was on holiday, a wet afternoon in a rented holiday home, miles from the nearest town, a cosy village not too far away, ideal for bike rides, walks and picnics in the summer. Once that thought embedded itself in her head she was unable to shift it. Life was one long holiday. That should be fun, but instead Ann found it unsettling. She would feel a jolt of panic as she worked in the garden or cleaned the kitchen, she would have to stop what she was doing and convince herself that she wasn't supposed to be somewhere else, doing something else. 'It's alright,' she told herself. 'You are in the right house, you are in the right place, relax.' But she remained unconvinced.

The second year was the real shock. The first winter they'd only just arrived and her relief at Harriet sleeping through the night was so overwhelming Ann barely noticed where she was. She started to come back to herself the following March, just as spring rushed the valley. It was small things at first. She would realise she was holding a cup of coffee, feel the shape of the handle in her hand, the weight of the drink in her wrist. The smell of the coffee caught her as if she hadn't smelt it for months. She would hear the slap of her bare feet on the bathroom tiles and notice the way her toes gripped the floor when it was wet after Harriet's bath. By the time the second winter hit, Ann was fully conscious and felt the brunt of it. The never-ending short days of darkness and cold. Even in the summer months it wasn't until the sun was midday-high before it beat the trees and lit the rooms, but from November to the end of February Ann felt like she was living underground. She bought lamps to bolster the light provided from the ceiling lights, and in the winter months she kept them on throughout the day, waging a war against the darkness. The house was fitted with central heating but the rooms were wide and tall and took a long time to warm up. Stepping out through the front door you were hit with a cold to make you reel, a cold that ached your teeth. The cold meant Ann didn't take Harriet and Daniel out much, and the more she didn't go out, the less she felt able to gather the energy to get the children into the car and go anywhere. And the trees. All those trees. They filed up to the garden in a line, they ran down either side of the house. There was a break at the front, but even then, just the narrow road, and they started again, a vast, deep wall in front of her.

They surrounded the house like soldiers, corralling every brick into place. She felt their presence, even in bed at night, standing over her, breathing, always watching. One night she dreamt of trees pushing up through the foundations and breaking through the floors into the kitchen and the lounge. In the morning she told Thomas about the dream and he smiled at her and said, 'How wonderful, trees in the house.' Ann shuddered at the thought and the dream stayed with her.

Ten

Etherton, 1989

Raymond was desperate for a phone call from Abbeystead. He was sure his house was crumbling by the day and living there triggered concern and worry that swarmed his chest like an angry mob, hijacked his thoughts and taunted him. He was positive there must be something catastrophically wrong with the house, looking at the state of it there must be, and it was only a matter of time before it collapsed in on him. At night he dreamt of water pouring through the roof, soaking him as he slept. And when he woke, as he did several times a night, his body was drenched, covered in a cold prickling sweat from his chest to his legs. When he jerked awake in panic, he worried what was happening to the house as he slept. Were the walls finally crumbling into nothing? Was the house sinking below street level? Taking the whole row down with it? Raymond needed work, fields underneath his feet, fells on the horizon. He needed a phone call from Abbeystead.

Etherton was wearying to him; litter collecting in the gutters, the same faces behind the same counters in the shops. But now, too, there was a new concern. A family had moved in next door. A man, a woman and two teenage girls. The day after they noisily appeared there was a loud knock at the front door. Raymond slowly pulled himself up from his bed and walked over to the window. He looked down onto the top of a shiny black head and ducked away just as the head turned its face upwards to the window.

'Anyone in?' the man shouted. 'Hello!' he bellowed.

Raymond retreated to the back wall of his bedroom and waited until the knocking and calling stopped. When he felt it was safe to do so, he walked back across the room, pushed his head to the wall and watched as the man strode up and down the street, talking to neighbours, talking to anyone who appeared. Smiling, shaking hands, patting backs. He was a short man, his mouth constantly on the verge of a forced-out smile. Raymond watched as the man spoke to more people in one afternoon than he spoke to in a year. He approached with his hand outstretched and the gruesome smile on his face. After shaking hands he would turn and point to his new home, then a bit more chat before he patted the men on the back, shook the women's hands again, bowing his head a little, before letting them on their way. Raymond was caught a few days later, returning from the shops. The man wore a brown leather jacket, his hair was slicked back, he looked ready for action, and when he saw Raymond he went for him.

'Mate!' he shouted from halfway down the street, just as Raymond pushed his key into the lock. 'Hang on mate!' He ran down the road, his short legs windmilling at an impressive speed.

Raymond froze with his arm holding the key in the lock.

'Keith, mate. Keith Sullivan,' he said, when he reached him, a little out of breath. 'New neighbour. I've been trying to say hello for days.'

He outstretched his arm and wriggled his fingers, twiddling for a handshake. Raymond offered his hand in return.

'Jesus, that's not a hand, that's a shovel!' he said as his hand disappeared into Raymond's grasp. 'Best not mess with you then.' He looked up at Raymond. 'How tall are you? Six four, six five?' he asked.

Raymond shrugged. He didn't know how tall he was. He couldn't remember ever being measured.

The man nodded. 'You are. Six four at least. Maybe even six five.'

The man funnelled his hands and shouted, 'What's the weather like up there?'

Raymond looked up at the sky and down at the little man and wondered if he was supposed to answer the question.

'Just moved in with the wife and girls,' he said, pointing at his house.

'Yes,' said Raymond.

'Seems like a good street. Friendly people, good town.'

'A good town,' Raymond said and nodded his agreement.

'Well, we won't cause you any trouble, and if you need anything, make sure you knock on.'

'Thank you,' said Raymond. He turned back to his door.

'You don't say much, do you pal?'

Raymond tried to smile a friendly smile at the man and turned his key in the lock.

'Sorry mate, I didn't get your name.' The man took a step closer.

'Raymond.'

'Raymond?'

'Farren.'

'Raymond Farren. Our new next-door neighbour. A right cheery sod.'

Raymond pushed open his door and stepped inside.

Raymond found that most people left him alone. He wasn't a rude man – when he was served in a shop he was polite; when conversation was unavoidable he did his best, but he was painfully shy and found people difficult. It had always been that way. When he was seven, the teacher told the class that everyone had to read a chapter of a book out loud, at the front of the room. The chapters were short and most of the children rattled through their reading in five minutes or less, the teacher trying to slow them down so the story could be heard and understood. Raymond's reading took half an hour. For the first five of those awful, excruciating minutes, he glanced over to Mrs Armitage, certain a reprieve must be coming at some point, but her face remained impassive throughout. When he finally pushed the last word of the final sentence out of his reluctant mouth, the children groaned in relief and Mrs Armitage said, 'Well done Raymond. I hope you've learnt a lesson today.'

The lesson Raymond had learnt was the fewer words the better. He decided not to speak unless it was impossible not to, and this seemed to work the majority of the time, most people seemed happy with it. He realised that people liked to talk, liked to be heard, so it was a good arrangement, he was one less competitor. But it didn't work with the family at number 13 who took a morbid fascination in Raymond and his quiet and awkwardness. The man cried out, 'Raymond mate!' whenever he saw him, showing him pictures of women in his newspaper, laughing when Raymond looked away. 'But you would though, wouldn't you? You'd have to, wouldn't you, given the chance?' he'd say, following Raymond down the street, staring at his paper. 'I'd break it in two.'

Keith was a nuisance but the daughters posed the real threat. One morning the knocking was so explosive, so insistent, that Raymond almost ran to the front door. He pulled the door open onto the two girls from number 13. They were smiling up at him.

'What are you doing?' the chubbier one asked.

Raymond shook his head. 'I'm not doing anything,' he said.

'You had to have been doing something,' the other one said. 'Even if you were just sitting down, that was doing something.'

'So what were you doing before you answered the door?' The first one again.

Raymond didn't know what to say, and the girl cupped her hand to her sister's ear and whispered. The sister swung her head away sharply and let out a huge squeal that filled the street and the sky. She stared at Raymond with a look of disgust. 'Oh God, you weren't, were you?' she asked, in pretend disbelief.

'We can hear you, you know. Through the wall,' the first one said, and started to grunt in a low voice, rubbing her knees as she did. The second one squealed again, grabbed her sister by the shoulder and they ran off down the street together, shouting terrible words about Raymond. Raymond closed the door and leant back into it. What he had been doing was lying on his bed, staring at the wall to his left. It was as close to doing nothing as he could get. They were right about the walls though; you could hear everything. He heard their TV, their rows and fights, the sex. He could even hear them in the bathroom. They were so loud, so much of the time, and so close, it felt like they were living with Raymond. Sometimes he worried that the whole family was about to burst through the thin wall and crash on top of him.

Raymond was stood in the kitchen the evening after the girls had knocked, gazing out at the back of the terraced houses that faced him, thinking about nothing, when the two girls jumped up from below his window, pummelled the glass and laughed at his shock. They clambered on his bin to escape, heaving themselves over the wall and into their own yard. They weren't remotely quick about it, but Raymond just stood and watched them go. What would he do if he caught them? He began to find litter on his doormat, his bin tipped over in the backyard almost every day. He knew not to answer the front door any more, but it didn't stop them knocking. And once they discovered his phone number a whole new world of fun opened up for them. But unlike the door, Raymond couldn't ignore the phone. And eventually, one morning in April, the call came and there were no screeching girls on the other end of the line, just the beautifully blunt farmer asking when he could get there. Raymond was in the caravan later that afternoon, his house locked up, abandoned. Let them do their worst. Sheila tapped on his door that evening. Raymond stood bent-backed in the small doorway as she explained that Chapman needed hospital treatment and they would require Raymond full-time for a while. 'Will that be alright?' she asked anxiously, her eyes darting around Raymond's large face. Raymond said that it was, and he hoped Chapman recovered well. He closed the caravan door quietly and his eyes filled quickly. He wiped the tears away but they returned in a second, and when his big shoulders started to shake he abandoned any resistance, lay down on the bed and wept. A week later Sheila drove Chapman away and Raymond carried out all his duties and Chapman's too. The work was wonderful. Exhausting. The list that Chapman had left could never be completed; even if he never came back it would go on and on. But Raymond didn't mind. Keep me going, he thought. Out here in Abbeystead, give me all the work you have.

Eleven

Keith Sullivan was a man who expected more from life. How he'd ended up broke, in a town like Etherton, with a wife he didn't love and two angry flat-footed teenage daughters, who seemed to despise him, was a daily shock. His first disappointment had been his stature. He was a short man, short verging on little. With encouragement from his mother he had expected to be much taller than his finished height. 'Your dad was a minnow until he was sixteen, then he shot up, there was no stopping him,' she told him many times, as he languished behind the other boys in his class, only coming up to the shoulders of the average-heighted lads. But sixteen came and went and brought no growth spurt for Keith, no aching legs and gangling unsteady limbs to control. He was still pushing himself up on his toes in photographs, looking for shoes that made him taller without showing a heel (even the hint of a heel drew mocking comments and focused attention on his shortness, he quickly found). It wasn't right – in Keith's head he didn't feel small and inconsequential; he felt like a man to be taken seriously, someone to be admired and envied. But then he would be queuing in a shop, staring at the shoulder blades of the woman in front of him, his nose almost tickled by the bottom of her ponytail. Or he would be pushing to get to a bar, stuck behind oversized men, their wide shoulders and heavy elbows barring his way. 'Sorry pal,' a large man might say, on noticing Keith, standing to one side, as if he was letting a cripple through. Keith finally gave up hope of any growth spurt at the age of twenty-one, and his mother finally learnt to be quiet about the late-flourishing height of his dead dad. She also learnt that Keith didn't like the saying 'Good things come in small packages', realising, eventually, that his broody silences and evil glares often coincided with her cheerful making of that point.

That he was only one good gene away from perfection frustrated Keith, gnawed away at him. He was a good-looking man. His hair was thick and dark and rested over a handsome face, and he dressed well – he had an eye for a good suit, a nice coat, a pair of quality shoes. He was particular about his clothes, particular about how they fitted. He couldn't bear for anything he owned to be too big, believing it drew attention to his diminutive status, so he took time to source clothes that fitted his frame perfectly. Or when that wasn't possible, which often it wasn't, his mother would cut and sew and adjust until he was happy. He would stand in front of the mirror before he went out and see the ideal man staring back at him. Handsome, well groomed, confident. But as soon as he stepped out of the door it would be confirmed that despite his good looks and good clothes, he was a foot too short for the world in front of him.

Keith disliked tall men and tall women equally. Big men made him feel daft; they made him queasy about himself. The dismissive glance of tall women pierced him for years. He could see that he was disregarded in the second it took to look him over. After years of knock-backs from taller women, and one occasion where the woman laughed when she realised Keith was, in fact, being serious with his offer, Keith reciprocated and ruled out tall women without a thought. Fuck them, he decided. Fuck them and their lanky legs and spindly arms, it would be like fucking a knitting needle anyway. He heard his mother's voice telling him, 'Good things come in small packages,' and, at least where it came to women, he began to accept it as truth.

The first thing Keith did on entering a room was to scan the horizon for heights before choosing where to place himself. He made a beeline for small men and women, and on the rare occasion he found a man shorter than himself he would stand next to him, to check that he was indeed the taller man, and a warm feeling would course through his body, making him feel like he'd drunk a good whisky by a warm fire on a cold night. The shorter man would find he had an ever so slightly taller shadow for the night.

Keith believed his shortness held him back. He knew that his life would have been different if he was only a few inches taller. He'd even read an article in the newspaper once, saying as much – tall men made more money and were more successful with women. Keith had often suspected that to be the case, but how cruel for someone to do the research and then print it out in black and white for the world to see. The report might have been cruel, but it was true – Keith had never had a good job, never kept one that long, and never earned much money. And the women he fell for never fell for him. Eventually, at twenty-eight, he married Rose Carpenter, who despite being only the same height as Keith and happy not to wear heels on a night out, was a disappointment to him. Rose had no money either and they settled down to a life of borderline poverty together. Eventually, after the bad jobs and daily frustrations took their toll, Keith couldn't contain the anger that sweated in his blood any more. He became the man who walked out of the pub with a smile for everyone he'd met that night and a bully at home, seeking revenge for the dismal failures he'd been forced to endure. Rose's small body absorbed these tantrums and rages over several years until she fought back one night, pulling a kitchen knife from a drawer. She pressed the point into Keith's neck until it began to pierce the skin and threaten an artery. Keith begged forgiveness, promising new behaviour. Killed by a wife he didn't particularly care for would be one humiliation too many.

It was inevitable, Keith felt, when he turned to crime. But he wasn't a very good criminal, his luck failed him quickly, and there were spells in prison. After his last stint inside Rose had agreed to take him back as long as he could find and keep a job. Keith had nowhere else to go in the world other than back to Rose, and reluctantly agreed to knuckle down. It was a friend of Rose's who managed to get him the position at Etherton Cement Works. His past was acknowledged by his new boss, who had seen trouble and escaped bad times himself, and it was agreed that if he could last six months turning up every day, doing the work with no cause for concern, the job would be his permanently. Keith surrendered to the offer. He found that the pay wasn't too bad, the work dirty and tiring but bearable. The family moved to Etherton and rented the small house on Granville Road. The house with a silent lumbering giant of a man next door. Keith couldn't believe it when he saw the size of the man clumsying down the street, the final pisstake – the tallest man in town living next door to the shortest. But Keith had made a deal with Rose to try this time, to get through the six months, go permanent, maybe get a bit more money. And then, when he had a steady stream of employment under his belt, he would have a look to see what else there was, see if he could find something more appealing than Etherton Cement Works. Maybe then he could move to a bigger house with a smaller neighbour.

Twelve

Thomas and Ann were fast asleep the night the petrol tank exploded outside the house. It was a hot night in a long series of hot nights and the bedroom window was wide open. The noise tore into the room and burst open above the bed. Thomas was wrenched awake and on his feet, peering through the window in seconds. He could see flames in the road. His heart pushed to escape the boundaries of his chest and his hands shook.

'What the hell was that?' Ann asked, following her husband to the window. But Thomas was already walking towards the bedroom door, adrenaline his motor.

'I don't think you should go outside, Thomas,' Ann said sharply.

'Somebody might be hurt,' he replied, his unsteady foot already on the first stair.

Thomas had seen flames from the bedroom window, and now he was on the road he could see clearly, a hundred yards away, the car, awash with fire, flames kicking and hissing, grabbing at the sky. Thomas ran forward, wondering why a car was burning here, knowing that if someone was inside there would be nothing he could do. He tried to prepare himself for a horrifying sight, came as close as the heat would allow and stared through the flames. He couldn't see anyone in there. He checked the back seats. He was sure there was nobody in there. He stepped back from the car, his face roaring hot, and looked around for someone connected to the fire, to the car. The lane was empty. Thomas turned to the car again, his brain searching itself for answers. He was thinking how it didn't make any sense when a large man burst out from the forest behind him shouting, 'Trees! Trees!'

Thomas nearly ran, but then he followed the direction of the man's jabbing finger and understanding shook him. The man was pointing at the top of the flames, at how close they were to the lower branches of the forest's dry trees.

'Fire engine!' the man shouted, just as Thomas turned to charge back to the house. As he ran he noticed how close the trees were to his home. Ann was right, they did surround the house, some branches almost touched the roof.

Thomas phoned the Fire Brigade and when he returned to the front door Ann called down the stairs. He looked up to see her standing with the children on the landing. 'It's a car. I can't see that anyone's hurt,' he said. 'But stay inside.' He didn't mention the high flames and the dry trees. Thomas stepped out of the front door to find the man there.

'Buckets?' the man said. 'Water?'

Thomas swore at his uselessness and ran back to the kitchen. He filled two buckets as quickly as he could and handed one to the man. Thomas walked awkwardly, moving as fast as he could without water lapping onto the road, but the big man shot away, carrying the full bucket as if it was an empty basket. They came as close as possible to the car and flung their water into the flames. The fire ate the water and the men pulled back from the heat.

'No point,' the man said and Thomas nodded his agreement. They could both see that the flames weren't quite as high any more anyway, that perhaps the danger had subsided.

They stood, holding their empty buckets, staring at the flaming car, and then Thomas held out his hand and said, 'Thomas Norton.'

The man looked at the hand, shook it, and said, 'Raymond Farren.'

In the light at the front of the house Thomas had seen the man more clearly and recognised him; he sometimes passed him on the lane, herding cattle to and from fields.

'You farm round here, don't you?' asked Thomas.

Raymond pointed in the direction and said, 'Nell Lane.'

They stood back and watched the car burn on.

Big wide lights eventually appeared on the road. The fire engine manoeuvred forward slowly, carefully, creeping its way through the dark, only just able to fit on the road. No siren marked its arrival, not even flashing lights. It pulled to a stop and the firemen clambered out, nobody in a rush at all, it seemed to Thomas.

'Teenagers,' a fireman told Thomas as his colleagues worked. 'Steal a car from one of the towns, race it to the middle of nowhere, destroy it by driving like an idiot, burn it up to leave no trace. Get a lift back home by a mate. We probably passed them on the way out here.'

'They come all the way out here?' Thomas asked.

'They've started to,' the fireman said. 'They can drive like idiots out here, no police around to stop them.'

Thomas shook his head and walked back to the house. He found Raymond sat at the kitchen table with a cup of tea, Ann making more drinks for the firemen, Daniel and Harriet buzzing around it all.

Thomas sat down with Raymond.

'The fireman said they steal a car and race it all the way out here . . .' he said, shaking his head.

The next day the corpse of the car was pulled onto the back of a truck and driven away. On his way back from work Thomas slowed as he passed the spot the car had burned. There were patches of glass in the road, oil stains on the tarmac, a chunk of melted bumper by the trees. He walked through the front door and shouted, 'Have you seen that? Out on the road? The mess?'

Ann was upstairs in their bedroom. She couldn't quite hear.

'They took the car away this morning,' she called back.

'But the state they've left it in,' Thomas shouted from the kitchen, his head under the sink, hunting out a bucket, a dust pan and scrubbing brush, any cleaning material he could find. He went through the side door into the garage for his tall wooden brush. Harriet followed him and asked, 'What are you doing, Daddy?'

‘I’m tidying the road up after last night, Harriet. I’m doing the job that should have been done by the men who collected the car.’

‘I’ll help,’ Harriet said, grabbing the bucket from him and skipping along behind her annoyed dad. But after ten minutes of road scrubbing she became bored and left Thomas to it. The stains on the tarmac were tricky, Thomas conceded, but he wanted them gone. He didn’t want to have to drive past such a mess every day, reminding him of the criminals who had visited, reminding him of the terror he’d felt, woken by an explosion. After twenty minutes on his hands and knees he’d scrubbed away most of the stains, but some dark patches remained, no matter how hard he worked. It would have to do for now, he decided; he needed a more powerful cleaning agent. He would ask at a local garage – they might be able to tell him what worked best on oil and petrol stains. Thomas glanced up and saw Ann outside the house, looking down the road to him. Still on his knees he waved a scrubbing brush at her. She paused for a moment before waving back and disappearing into the house.

Thirteen

Ann had fallen in love a year before she met Thomas. She was sixteen, it was summer, and she felt stifled. She spent long hours in her bedroom listening to albums she'd listened to hundreds of times, attempting to read novels she thought she should read, but nothing connected, none of it cut through the fug surrounding her. Her friends were moping around their own houses too, and every few days they would meet in one house and mope together. Everyone complained about being bored, but it wasn't just boredom Ann felt, it was lifelessness. She felt stunted. She was sixteen, the world should finally have been opening up to her, but instead she felt trapped in a sealed pod with just enough air to keep her alive. Everything in her life was muffled – her quiet parents, the stuffy house, even her friends had begun to bore and frustrate her. But unlike her friends, who were prepared to wait out the long summer in dull houses until A levels began, Ann was impatient; she wanted something to happen now. One afternoon, with her mum upstairs taking her afternoon nap, she spent a silent hour staring at the ugly ornaments on the mantelpiece in the dining room and decided to act. She walked straight into the town and began asking for jobs. The Black Horse was the first pub she tried and the first place to offer her any work.

During her first shift Ann was concentrating on taking the right food to the right tables and not spilling anything on anyone. She didn't notice the dark-haired barman watching her every hesitant move. But as her confidence grew she felt the eyes following her, from the kitchen to the tables and back again, and towards the end of the night she met the eyes confidently. She had to look away quickly, worried she would laugh. Conner Ryan was twenty and beautiful. Ann had seen men like him in adverts, selling aftershave or modelling watches with a haunted stare, but this man was only five feet away and working behind a bar in Maltham. She looked again, to make sure, and when he smiled at her, she spluttered, and said, 'God, sorry,' and rushed back to the kitchen, hoping to hide until she regained her composure.

They had only been out once when Conner turned

up at the house late on a Thursday night. George Stead stumbled down the stairs and opened the door, his dressing gown thrown hastily over his pyjamas.

'Is Ann about?' Conner had asked, sweeping back his helmet-squashed hair with his hand.

'About? It's half past eleven on a Thursday night and she's sixteen. She's in bed. Asleep.'

Conner smiled at Ann's dad, nodded behind him and said, 'A sleepwalker, is she?'

Ann hadn't been asleep, she'd heard the motorbike approach and would have answered the front door long before her dad if she hadn't been wearing ancient pink pyjamas, dotted with white petal heads. She'd hurriedly changed into jeans and a top and rushed down the stairs, mortified to find her dad, who looked older than she'd ever seen him look; his hair ruffled by sleep, a confused expression on his face, holding his arm across the doorframe as if Conner was threatening an assault on the house.

'Ann?' he said, when she arrived at his side.

'It's a friend from work, Dad. We'll just be five minutes. I promise.'

Her dad looked from Conner to Ann and back to Conner. 'Five minutes,' he said, tapping his naked wrist and slowly mounting the foot of the stairs, glancing back distrustfully at the handsome young man at his front door. Ann felt the relief of waking from a falling dream when he finally turned the corner onto the landing and disappeared from sight. She stepped out of the front door and hissed at Conner, 'What are you doing here?'

Conner dragged her to him and kissed her. Ann returned the kiss and then pulled away, slapping Conner's arm before letting her body fall back into his arms. It was thrilling to be held by him.

'I wanted to see you,' he said, holding her tightly, pushing his hands into the small of her back as if trying to meld her into him. They kissed again and held each other. Ann was sure that nobody in Maltham had ever felt how she felt just then. Certainly not her parents, or any of her parents' friends. And not any of her own friends. How could they have? She knew these people – how could they have felt like this and still look and act the way they did?

Conner was facing the house. 'So this is the Stead mansion,' he said.

'It's hardly a mansion.' Ann sounded more defensive than she meant to.

'It's a mansion where I come from.' Conner ran his hands deeply through Ann's hair, starting at the roots and finishing at the freshly cut tips, then he kissed her gently on the neck, climbed onto his motorbike and roared away, messing up the gravel drive as he tore off. Ann waved him away and listened to the high rip of the engine gradually fade until all that was left was the silence of late-night Maltham. Ann was electrified – all her summer boredom was gone. Even the stale house behind her seemed full of possibilities, the familiar garden in front of her, where a couple of years before she'd practised handstands and cartwheels, looked promising and mysterious in the dark evening. Before she turned to step back into the house, to return to her room and think about Conner, Ann looked at the disturbed drive and wondered if her dad would rake the gravel smooth before he left for work or when he returned. She guessed correctly and by the time she was awake the next morning the drive was as smooth as if Conner had never visited. She would never be like that, she decided. She could never be that tragic.

Ann fell in love quickly, and not just because of Conner's looks, although her friends never quite believed that, but because he was so full of all the life that was absent from every room in her parents' house. If he wasn't working in the pub, he was on the other side of the bar, if he wasn't drinking in the pub, he was off somewhere else, seeing someone else, planning something else. And his sleeves were always rolled up. Ann didn't know why she liked that so much, but she realised one hot afternoon as she watched her dad mowing the back lawn from her bedroom window, with his shirt tucked into his trousers, his cuffs buttoned down at his wrists: she couldn't remember a single time she'd ever seen her dad's arms. Her parents didn't say a word about the relationship. She imagined the conversation between them – her mum telling her dad to let it run its course, that the worst thing they could do would be to forbid; it would only make Ann more determined. So the relationship was tolerated at home, not that they ever spent any time there. They were always out. Conner's world became Ann's in a matter of weeks.

Ann knew her friends were jealous. They were left choosing from the sixth-form boys whilst she was riding on the back of Conner Ryan's motorbike, going to parties on the other side of town, drinking in his favourite pubs, how could they not be jealous? She heard them talking one day when she was sat outside an open window of the common room.

'He's so affected,' Juliette said.

'I know, he gives me the creeps,' Angela said.

'And it's not as if he's that good-looking,' Juliette

again. 'I think his chin is too big to be honest and that smile makes him look simple. And there's no way he's faithful to her. Someone like that, working in a pub all the time.'

Ann stood up, swung her bag over her shoulder, strode into the common room and said, 'Hello girls!' as brightly as she could, and watched as they rushed to smile and wave her over. Juliette had the gall to pat the free seat next to her. Ann paused, but went and sat. She couldn't bring herself to care.

It lasted a year. Ann had even stopped questioning why Conner was with her and not one of the other waitresses or one of the girls who came in the pub to drool over him. She'd finally learnt to accept that Conner was in love with her. Weeks after she dropped her guard, he crushed her heart. She was with Juliette, they were on a study period walking to a cafe in the middle of town when they heard the distinctive high-pitched wail of Conner's bike heading towards them over Church Brow. Ann couldn't quell the excitement she felt in her stomach, the light-headedness she still experienced when she knew she would be seeing him. He crested the brow of the hill looking glorious, the sun and blue sky behind him like a cinema screen, but something was wrong with the picture. Ann didn't understand what until the bike had almost passed her. On the back of the bike, where Ann always sat, was a blonde girl, her arms wrapped around Conner's waist, her hair flapping across the front of her visor, Ann's visor, whipping the back of Conner's neck. He didn't slow, he didn't look at Ann, and then he was gone.

Juliette turned to Ann and said, 'Fuck! Ann, are you alright?' She was unable to suppress a giddy grin.

'I'm fine,' Ann said. 'It was probably just a friend from the pub.' She stalked off to the cafe, but when she lifted the coffee cup to her lips five minutes later she found that her hands were shaking.

If she'd seen it coming it wouldn't have been so bad. Even a hint of a warning and she could have prepared herself, but the way she was dropped was brutal. Conner wouldn't return her calls, swapped his shifts at the pub, and, if he couldn't swap, barely acknowledged her at all. She longed to talk to him, to find out what she'd done wrong, to see if she could make it better, but Conner wouldn't tolerate her approaches. When she cried he simply walked away. She realised she was becoming the laughable ex-girlfriend, pitied by his friends, mocked by the new girlfriend, and fought every instinct that told her to run to him, throw herself at his feet and beg him to take her back. Ann couldn't bear to have her mum fussing, or her dad being obviously kind, so she cut them dead as soon as they looked like broaching the subject. It was more difficult with her friends, who were dying to talk endlessly, unable to conceal the satisfaction they felt at Ann being dropped and shunted back to them in such a remorseless way. Ann started to avoid them. She preferred to suffer without spectators. Heartbreak shocked her. She thought about visiting the doctor at one point, so physically she felt the pain she began to confuse it with illness. She cried in her bedroom in the mornings and evenings and, when needed, in the toilets at the sixth form. In public she displayed a stoic face.

'You're doing very well,' her mum said to her three weeks after Conner had stopped visiting and calling. Ann shrugged the comment away dismissively. 'I'm fine,' she snapped and walked off. Her parents and friends thought Ann was fully recovered months before she could drag herself out of bed without feeling heartbroken, humiliated and exhausted. She read *The End of the Affair* in secret in her room, her hands shaking as she turned the pages, her heart aching with desperate recognition. If only she'd read it before she met Conner, she wouldn't have acted so recklessly, so carefree, so bloody stupidly. And all those bloody classes over all those years at school and nobody ever mentioned, nobody warned you or taught you to be careful, that heartbreak could tear you down.

Fourteen

Raymond ate his tea with the Chapmans and listened to Sheila relay the gossip she'd picked up on her visit to the village. She obviously hadn't heard about the exploding car, or else she would have mentioned it. Sheila loved any trouble or wrongdoing; an affair in Abbeystead kept her eyes sparkling and her mouth busy for months. But today she stuck to the meagre gossip she'd managed to uncover and Chapman grunted his responses to her small revelations, commenting only when money was brought into the conversation.

'How much?'

'That's what she told me.'

'Who?'

'Ainsworth.'

'We're in the wrong business, clearly.'

After helping Sheila with the dishes Raymond returned to his caravan and sat on the bed. He'd already decided he wouldn't go night-walking that evening; he was tired from the events of the night before, he hadn't slept until almost dawn.

Raymond had been a mile under the trees when he first heard the engine noise. He was unsure initially, it was a distant buzz, a small fly in the corner of a large room, but the sound grew louder and like sickness in the body it eventually revealed itself as unmistakably present. The noise swarmed around him, a mile to the left, to the north, and then behind him. The persistent intrusion brought to mind the two girls from number 13 and Raymond turned to head back towards his caravan. The cars had been coming recently at night, racing the forest roads, engines straining, and Raymond hated it. The noise unsettled him, it sounded sinister and dangerous, out of control. Raymond decided he would get himself home and lock the caravan door, something he only did when he heard cars in the forest. He was confused when he heard the explosion – all had been quiet for a while and he thought the car might have left for good. It was with reluctance he began to lumber his way to the source of the noise. He didn't want anything to do with the trouble he was running towards, but he knew that someone might need help, and if he heard later that a young lad had died, alone in a wreck, the thought that he'd not helped would haunt him. Raymond didn't swear, but as he pushed himself through the trees he said, 'Fucking hell,' out loud. 'Fuck, fucking hell.'

It was the woman who'd dragged him indoors, Ann he thought she'd said her name was. He felt a pull of guilt at the memory of all his previous visits years before as he was shown into the house and ushered into the kitchen. Children were running around, firemen came and went, drinks were made and handed out. It was a commotion that was alien to Raymond. He sat at the kitchen table in the middle of it all and tried to keep up with what was being said. And then suddenly everyone was outside and he was alone with his drink. He walked into the hallway and glanced into the front room. The house was beautiful. The carpets thick and soft, the walls smooth and clean. He hoped he wasn't making a mess; he checked his feet for mud and sniffed himself, to see if he smelt too much of the farm. He was as careful as possible with his drink, sure he would spill some. He downed the last of his tea with a gulp, returned to the kitchen, washed his cup and slipped out of the house, into the trees and back towards his caravan without anyone seeing. He fell asleep not thinking of burning, abandoned cars but warm houses, flat walls, soft carpets and clean smells. That was what he was thinking of now, back in the caravan again, remembering the house. He knew some people lived like that, of course he did, he'd seen pictures in magazines, programmes on television, but he'd never been in a house like that before. The Chapman farmhouse, whilst far removed from his own squalid home, still had frayed carpets, thin curtains, and dark rooms which needed decorating. In the Nortons' house there were no odd chairs, no chipped cups. Everything was solid and expensive, everything had been chosen because it fitted the room and house. It pleased Raymond to see a family living there happily. He couldn't help imagining what it would be like to wake up in one of the bedrooms, walk barefoot on those soft carpets to the bathroom in the morning. The parents probably had an en suite bathroom in their bedroom, he thought. Imagine that. In the mornings, at home, Raymond walked on cold, ratty floors to a freezing, ancient bathroom where he washed his body as quickly as he could at the sink. On the farm he had to brave all kinds of weather and rush across to the farmhouse for his allotted few minutes. But imagine waking up and walking a few steps to a bathroom in your own bedroom.

Showering in hot water, drying yourself with a soft, clean towel and then stepping back onto deep carpet to get dressed. What a way to start the day.

Fifteen

As far back as when they were heading towards the burning car with buckets of heavy water Thomas knew that he would call round to see Raymond to say thank you. He felt it was important to acknowledge kindness, to show appreciation, and he was thankful that Raymond had run out from the trees and shaken him from his inactivity. But there was an ulterior motive. The night had shaken Thomas, upset him, and he wanted someone to talk to. He couldn't talk to Ann; he was sure that she'd enjoyed the commotion, enjoyed the busy house and he didn't trust her to understand how he'd been feeling. The next morning, when he was tired and irritable, he was met by a bright and bouncy Ann in the kitchen, chatting away with the children about the fire engine, the explosion, the naughty men from the town who'd stolen the car. The episode seemed to cheer her up whilst Thomas had been heavy with worry since that night. Before the burning car he'd never considered the possibility of crime in Abbeystead, he believed the further away from towns and cities, the safer you were. But now he saw vulnerability in their remoteness. They were further away from criminals, that was probably true, but they were also further away from help, and Thomas had been made to realise that criminals travelled. He wanted to talk about it. To a man who could reassure him. A local.

He knew Raymond's farm on Nell Lane, it was only two miles away, just outside the forest. It was a week after the fire when Thomas drove up the bumpy track in his Land Rover, driving slowly over cattle grids, keeping a close eye on the sheep which scattered recklessly in front of him in disorganised bursts. He reached the farmhouse and parked next to a dirtier, older Land Rover. A woman with stiff short hair and the face of a mole opened the front door. Squinting into the light she said, 'Are you here for Frank?'

Thomas was sure he'd heard the man say 'Raymond', but it had been a strange night, the man had spoken softly and he was at the only farm on Nell Lane. He must have misheard. He was about to explain who he was and why he was there when the woman turned and bellowed for Frank.

‘Come in,’ she said, standing back. She led the way down a dark corridor. ‘I’m Sheila, Frank’s wife.’

She bawled for Frank again and this time a short, balding, red-faced man, in his fifties at least, appeared from a room at the bottom of the murky corridor. The two men met in the narrow space and Thomas felt ridiculous, he’d come to the wrong house somehow.

‘Sorry,’ Thomas said, ‘I must have got the wrong farm. I was looking for a different man.’ Thomas raised his hand in front of him like a forklift, ‘A big man, brown hair.’

‘Raymond,’ Sheila and Frank said together.

‘That’s it,’ said Thomas, relieved, ‘Raymond.’

‘You’ll need the caravan round the back then. He’s already had his tea.’ Sheila flapped Thomas back the way he’d come and when he stepped out of the front door she waved her hand and said, ‘Right round the back, past the sheds, past the shippen, you’ll find him in his caravan there.’ Sheila watched Thomas go. He was Raymond’s first ever visitor.

Thomas found the caravan at the edge of a field behind the outbuildings. He knocked on the door and Raymond appeared high above him, the caravan adding an extra foot to his height.

'I wanted to say thank you,' said Thomas, pushing a hand forward and up, 'for your help the other night. For bringing me to my senses.'

'I was out walking,' Raymond said, quickly. 'I don't sleep well and I like to walk.'

Thomas nodded, his hand still outstretched. Ann had wondered what Raymond had been doing in the forest at night, but Thomas couldn't understand her thinking. Criminals had stolen a car, set fire to it outside their house, it had exploded and Ann was worried about a local farmer who'd been nearby to help. Her thinking made no sense.

'I like the forest. Even at night,' Raymond added. He didn't offer a hand so Thomas withdrew his.

'I do my walking in the morning,' Thomas said. 'Usually before seven.'

Raymond filled the caravan door, his head and torso sticking out into the air. Thomas could see that the caravan was too small for Raymond to ask him in, and it wouldn't feel right anyway, two strangers in an intimate space, the space where a man slept. Thomas thought that he should leave, but he wanted more than a ten-second chat at the door of a caravan. He'd envisaged the pair of them sat in a farmhouse kitchen, drinking tea as they went over the details of what had happened the night of the fire.

'Well, I wanted to say thank you,' said Thomas, again. 'I was glad you were there to help.'

Raymond said, 'Right,' and looked over Thomas's shoulder, his eyes narrow as if assessing the incoming weather. Thomas dangling, grasping for something, anything, pulled his head back and said, 'You don't fancy a short walk now do you?'

Raymond stepped down from the caravan and pulled the door shut behind him and began to walk. Thomas, left behind for a moment, started off after him. They were heading to the trees.

They walked in silence for a few minutes until Thomas said, 'We've been here for nearly seven years now. I can't believe it's been that long already.'

'Do you like it?' Raymond asked.

'Never been happier,' Thomas said, as he followed Raymond's lead through the trees. 'Until the other night anyway. That threw me to be honest. Shook me up a little.'

Raymond nodded vigorously and Thomas, encouraged, carried on. 'I didn't expect any trouble out here, I thought we'd left that behind in the town.'

'They've been coming though,' said Raymond.

The words were an icy blanket on Thomas's shoulders. He wanted to be told that Abbeystead was a haven, free from crime. He wanted to hear that the incident from the previous night was a one-off, that Raymond had never heard anything like it before. He thought for a few seconds.

'We haven't had any trouble before, nothing in all the years,' he said.

'They've been coming these last few months. You might not get it so much down your road – they like the faster roads.'

'You hear them from your caravan, do you?'

Raymond nodded. 'I don't like it,' he said. 'They shouldn't come.'

Thomas was pleased to hear a man talking sense.

'They shouldn't come,' he agreed, 'it's not right.'

They walked up a steep incline and at the top, when they stopped for breath, Thomas asked, 'Do you live in the caravan?'

'When I'm working I do.'

'So you aren't here all the time then?'

'Just when they need me, when there's work.'

'So where is home?'

'I have a house over in Etherton, the other side of Eldpen Hill.'

Thomas nodded, he knew Etherton. He'd driven a colleague home a couple of times. It was a rundown town, he remembered. A dismal place. People waiting for buses which would surely never come. In his memory it was raining.

'I prefer it here,' Raymond said.

Thomas agreed. 'Yes, well there can't be many places as beautiful as this. As undisturbed as this. Abbeystead is a gem.'

'Best place in the world!' said Raymond with a gusto that surprised Thomas.

'We love it out here,' said Thomas, ignoring the fact that he'd spent the last few years realising that Ann probably didn't love it at all. 'So much nature, so much space for the kids. They're free to come and go as they please. A proper childhood.'

'Yes,' agreed Raymond, 'a proper childhood.'

'And the views. The views you get at every turn,' Thomas said.

They walked on through the trees, naming more and more things they liked about Abbeystead.

Sixteen

Thomas was right – Ann didn't love Abbeystead. It felt to her a place on the edge, a place removed from the pulse of the world. Abbeystead wasn't visited like the valleys an hour further north in the Lake District, there weren't cars turning off the motorway in their thousands on weekends and bank holidays. Locals claimed that Abbeystead was a 'hidden gem', that it wasn't more popular because it was tucked away below the obvious attractions of the Lakes, but Ann didn't believe that was the reason large numbers didn't come. From the right vantage point, in the right weather, Abbeystead was undeniably impressive, but there was to Ann's eye a bleakness to the landscape, a functionality. On a cold winter's day with the trees stripped and black, the fells grey and distant, the wind cavorting recklessly around the valley, it seemed to her that Abbeystead was a stranded bruise of a place. At least in Maltham there had been people. 'All this rain,' a neighbour would say when they passed on the street, 'we'll have to build an ark soon.' Pointless, everyday, nothing communication, but Ann missed it. She could go for days without that type of interaction in Abbeystead. A quick wave from another forest dweller as they carefully negotiated their cars past each other on thin roads was the most she could hope for on most days. And if you don't see people every day, if you don't start off by saying the small, obvious things, how do you end up saying more and becoming friends, or even enemies? Despite Thomas and the children, Ann was lonely. It seemed that she and Thomas had run out of things to say to one another shortly after they'd moved into the barn. The months before the move had been fraught. They were dealing with Harriet's screaming, and buying and converting the barn. And then, unbelievably, the barn was finished, they moved in, Harriet fell quiet, and there was nothing left to say. Thomas was lost in his thoughts, wandering his beautiful Abbeystead, and Ann felt parachuted into a place that didn't feel anything like home.

Children weren't a cure for loneliness. They stood outside the equation. In the mornings, at breakfast, before Ann had full control over her thoughts, she sometimes felt the embarrassment of a stranger in front of Daniel and Harriet. She busied herself pouring drinks, dishing out cereal, wiping surfaces clean, feeling like a nanny to the two good-looking children in front of her.

Some days Daniel was almost impossible.

'Would you like toast, Daniel?'

A nod or a shake.

Later on in the day, 'How was school, Daniel?'

A shrug, a muttered 'Fine.'

'Don't forget your favourite programme is on later, Daniel.'

'I hadn't forgotten.'

He was the same with Thomas – short answers, impatient, bordering on insolent.

'He's just shy,' was Thomas's theory, 'a quiet lad.'

But Ann knew that not to be the case. She'd seen him in the school yard, the other children running up to him as he arrived, deferring to him, offering him sweets, keen to win his approval. He wasn't shy.

Ann felt more guilt over her feelings for Harriet. 'Isn't she adorable,' was the most likely comment from people when they first met Harriet. And Harriet's round cheeks, big smile and long brown hair all combined to make her unimpeachably adorable. But sometimes Ann couldn't help finding her daughter's behaviour cloying. She wanted her to misbehave now and then – to throw a tantrum, lie or steal, slap and scratch, but she never did. Even when ill she was stoic and unfussy. 'Don't worry about me, Mummy, I'll be fine,' she said in the middle of a brutal vomiting bout that had been tearing through the school and finally caught Harriet. Ann couldn't equate the happy little girl Harriet had become with the screaming bundle of terror that had arrived in their lives a few years before and sent them scurrying to the trees. Her children seemed so much more settled and rooted than her. They didn't appear to mind the large dark house under the branches, the long car journeys it took to get anywhere, the grey fells and black streams, the gloomy emptiness of the place.

It was a shock to Ann, the way she felt about her children. She'd always wanted to be a mother and even as a school girl, when one of her friends would say, 'God that's disgusting, pushing something the size of that out of yourself,' her arms spread wide to indicate a baby the size of a television, and everyone would shriek at the horror and impossibility of it, Ann would shriek too, but she wanted children, was certain of it. And whilst she had fears about what would happen to her body and the pain of childbirth, she didn't worry that she would struggle with motherhood – it never crossed her mind. When pregnant with Daniel her concern was that she would love too much, worry about the child all the time, worry to distraction, smother with attention. When a car sped past she shuddered and held her pregnant belly and fretted about the day her child would be old enough to walk along pavements by busy roads without her supervision. And now the children were here she did love them, she would die for them, but it wasn't the feeling of all-encompassing love she'd been expecting. Ann was shocked at how quickly she was bored with motherhood, particularly when Daniel was very young, by his demands for attention, his neediness and endless presence. 'He never goes away!' she wanted to shout at people when they came to visit and cuddle and coo. 'He's here all the time!'

But the plan had always been for two children and how could she tell Thomas that she wasn't even sure she was handling one child well. What would he think of her if she told him that sometimes she wished Daniel wasn't there? And maybe, anyway, she just needed to get used to motherhood. Perhaps she just needed more time to adjust. And then, of course, along came Harriet and her terror and lungs, and

Ann was dreaming of a return to the days of tedium and boredom with Daniel. With Harriet, for the first year, it was about survival, nothing more, and somehow they did survive, and then, one day, Ann drove both children to school and drove home in an empty car to an empty house. It was a day she'd been waiting for, dreaming about. Six hours without children, six hours, every day, five days a week. It was a luxury she could hardly comprehend. They had spoken about a job, her and Thomas, but Thomas liked things as they were, enjoyed the rhythms and routines of their life. And he was earning reasonably well, they weren't an extravagant family, their spending was modest. 'What about holidays and sickness?' he asked. 'How will we cover those?' So they agreed Ann would look for something suitable in a few years, when the children were older.

Ann didn't intend to waste a moment of the time afforded her. She remembered the minutes, hours and days she'd let slip away before she'd had children. Time spent doing so little when she could have been doing so much. There were courses to study, books to read, friends to catch up with. In fact, what couldn't be achieved with thirty free hours a week? But when the time came, when the hours were laid out in front of Ann, she froze. She thought at first that she was disabled by the freedom given to her; that she was so worried about wasting a second of time she was paralysed into inactivity. Ann would start a book and put it down after four pages, distracted by worry – was it the right book to be reading now? Should she be reading another book instead? She would flick through the prospectus for the Open University, wondering what to study – should it be something purely for enjoyment or a course that would help her find a better job when the time came? Ann would consider visiting a friend to shake her out of her slump, but they lived too far away now just to drop in, she would need to phone first, and her hand didn't reach for the phone. The first few free weeks passed in a muddle of frustrated anxiety, of books started and discarded, courses considered and rejected, trips never taken. And then suddenly, without warning, it was winter. The leaves fell, there were brief days of sharp autumn sun, warm air held in a dizzying chill frame, and then it was winter. Short dark days of cold and rain. Ann found it hard to even move. She'd begun her free time sluggishly, but now she was disabled. She would drive the children to school in the murky mornings and return to the house, the trees stealing the miserly light the day was offering. The house would be cold and dark on her return and it took a monumental effort to keep on top of the housework, never mind attempt anything else. If she forced herself the housework could be finished by lunch and after eating she would try to read one of the many books borrowed from the library but would invariably drift into sleep with the book dropped into her lap. When she woke the house would be even darker than before, she would feel the trees outside, lined up against her, and she wanted to run.

Seventeen

Keith didn't last the required six months. The odds were against him from the outset – he'd never lasted six months in any job. And this job was tiring, exhausting at times, so when he woke up blinded by pain, racked with sickness, he didn't bother turning up because he couldn't have done the work anyway. Hungover to the point of useless was how he woke quite often in his first months in Etherton. Boredom was his downfall. Work, eat, sleep, shit wasn't enough. He needed some excitement, and that led him to drink. But he wasn't interested in just being drunk, it was the ritual of the night out he loved. The shower after tea and then choosing the clothes, laying them out on the bed to check the outfit worked, the careful dressing and slapping on of aftershave, the ten minutes spent in front of the mirror combing his hair until it was a perfect sweep on his head. Then into the night. The possibilities stretching out in front of him, even in a town like Etherton. The first drinks were always the best, the last drinks an effort to get back to the hope and promise of the earlier drinks, and whilst that didn't always work, sometimes it did. On those nights Keith would fall asleep feeling euphoric, full of plans, his promised future twinkling like lights on the sea front. And then he would wake up with the pain of the hangover and the disappointment of remembering who he was and where he was, the reality of the dull day lined up in front of him, with all its sisters and brothers waiting dourly behind.

It was Rose's fault Keith was sacked, he believed. If she'd let him stay in bed, he would still have a job, but the day he was fired Rose pulled the bed sheets off him at seven in the morning. 'You,' she said, poking him sharply in his neck, 'are going to work.' In the early hours Keith had returned from a heavy session, woken Rose up and demanded she cook him something to eat. When she refused a huge row had followed which culminated in the whole family screaming at Keith and Keith throwing a bedside table down the stairs in blind fury. With the sheets torn off him, a sore neck and nowhere to hide, Keith stumbled to the bathroom, where he was sick into the sink. He sat on the toilet for half an hour, trembling and sweating, regretting every drink. When Rose began pounding on the door he went to change into his work clothes, wanting to get out of the house, away from the mad, nagging woman. Despite having to stop on the way to work to be sick again Keith found himself thirty minutes early for his shift. He curled himself up on the bench in the corner of the Portakabin where the men hung their coats, ate their lunch and fell asleep. Keith woke when a couple of colleagues came noisily through the door. He kept his sore head down, his arms wrapped around himself and his eyes closed so he wouldn't have to engage in any conversation.

'Look at him over there,' one of the men said, 'curled up asleep like a little dormouse.'

'Bit small for a dormouse that one,' the other man said.

Keith wasn't lying on the bench any more. He was a whirling ball of arms and legs, careering towards the men as fast as a spinning wheel. Just as he launched his attack Eric Calpin, Keith's boss, came through the door. He helped drag Keith off his shocked colleague and pinned him against the wall with the other men. The smell of drink fled from Keith's pores, violent words crashed from his mouth, he struggled and thrashed like a rat in a bag. It was five minutes before the three men felt able to remove their hands from him, to let him down off the wall. It was the quickest firing Eric had ever been involved with and Keith, by then spent and still unwell, went calmly, meekly, not shocked he'd lost another job, just relieved he could go home and back to bed.

The next morning Rose stripped the bed of its covers again and demanded Keith get dressed and go and find some work. 'I got you this job. We moved the whole family here, and don't think we're going back to living off nothing. We're not living off my cleaning money, Keith. Not the amount those two eat and the amount you drink.'

Keith was happy to escape Rose's fury but the streets of Etherton quickly turned his mood sour and then black. It would be better to be poor somewhere else, he thought. With cash in your pocket Etherton wasn't so bad; there were pubs and shops like anywhere else. Without money it was a shithole. He idled through the streets, trying to ignore the regret that was spreading like a virus in his chest, draping itself over his shoulders. Eventually there were no more streets to walk and Keith braced himself and climbed up the steep steps and into the job centre. He scanned the cards on the board and immediately saw that the best paid jobs were at the cement works. He even saw his own job advertised already. After discounting the cement jobs he was left with shop assistant, kitchen hand or factory work. All so low paid it wasn't worth it, all jobs for younger men. An image of himself as an old man alone in a bedsit in a tall dark house jumped into his head. He shivered and flung the thought away. He turned and assessed the women behind the desks on the far side of the room. They all looked hard-faced and battle-ready and he was in no mood. His sacking would complicate signing on and they would insist he applied for the useless jobs pinned to the board. Keith fingered his wallet – there was still £60 from his last wage packet in there. He left the job centre and went to the cheap cafe by the station and cradled a cup of sweet tea until the pubs opened.

Keith knew the pubs well at night, but daytime drinking was a different scene. He tried the Swan and the Brown Cow first, but they were both dead, nothing more than a bored landlord in either. Keith knew there must be life somewhere, there always was, you just had to seek it out. He found it in the Victoria, a small low-ceilinged pub at the side of an alley opposite the library. There were three small rooms, each one with men sitting, smoking, drinking and talking. The smoke hovered in the air, there were cigarette burns like bullet holes in the upholstery and the mottled glass windows meant nobody could see in from the outside. Keith liked it. He climbed on a bar stool, ordered a pint and arranged his change on the bar top. Over the next couple of pints he chatted to the barman, and to the men, as they came and ordered their drinks, stared ahead as if lost in thought when there was nobody to talk to. Keith knew how to be absorbed into a community of drinkers – it was simple. You stayed in the same spot, not pushing yourself on anyone, you commented when required, agreeing with whatever point of view held sway, you accepted the offer of a drink if it came and always bought one back. By the end of the afternoon he was part of a group of men sat in the back room of the pub. Keith had told the men he'd come to Etherton for the job at the cement works and, with a few omissions and alterations, the story of his sacking. For the last half an hour the men had shared similar stories of terrible jobs and unreasonable bosses and Keith was enjoying himself. He was sad when everyone began dribbing and drabbing out of the pub, making way for the after-work drinkers. Keith found himself alone with a blond man called

John and they stayed for an extra couple of drinks together. He liked John, he was a few years younger than Keith and he let him talk, let him tell his stories. He laughed at the funny moments and acted angry for Keith when there was reason to be angry. Keith was sad when John stood up to leave, he'd been thinking they might drink on into the night, but John said, 'See you Thursday? We meet around two on Tuesday and Thursdays.' Keith was non-committal, but he was already looking forward to Thursday.

Thursday went the same way with Keith and John left alone at the end of the afternoon. Keith drained his glass and despite wanting to stay, and John showing no signs of being ready to leave, gathered his change together and said that he'd be off.

'Stay for another,' John said, but Keith shook his head. The £60 in his wallet was almost gone and he didn't know when any more money would find its way there to replace it.

'Have you got somewhere to be?' John asked.

Keith shook his head. 'I'm a bit broke at the minute,' he admitted. 'Down to my last bean is the truth.'

'It happens,' John said, 'it happens to all of us.'

Keith wondered what John did for money. Despite

claiming to have known poverty, his wallet was always full, he wasn't rooting in his pocket for coins when he approached the bar. What job paid so well and let you spend afternoons in the pub?

'Let me shout you a drink,' John said.

Keith held up his hand to protest, but in his head he was already drinking the drink. John returned from the bar with a pint and whisky for each of them, dismissing Keith's thanks.

'We all have our ups and downs,' he said, as he carefully slid the drinks onto the table. 'And it's important to share when you happen to be going through a green patch.'

Keith nodded firmly at this. As if his ups had ever come along half as regularly as his downs. As if he would share. He took a glass and drank a big swig of beer.

'I'm expecting some work to come along soon,' John said, 'if you'd be interested?'

Keith looked up from his drink, suddenly alert. 'Anything would be good,' he said.

'Let me speak to the other two, see what they say. I know they're looking for an extra man for a job they have in mind.'

John took a glug from his pint, threw the whisky into himself and stood up to leave.

'See you Tuesday. We'll discuss it then.'

They shook hands and John left the pub. Keith looked at the near full pints and the whisky in front of him and smiled.

Eighteen

Thomas and Raymond met on Tuesday evenings at the side of the forest by the farm. They usually headed into the trees, but sometimes they drove to the foot of a hill and climbed to the summit, or walked across Chapman's fields to Steadlow reservoir. Raymond knew every tree, plant, flower and shrub they came across, and didn't need prompting after a while. 'Pink campion,' he would say as they passed a cluster of small-headed, pinky-red flowers gathered around a tree trunk. Thomas would make a mental note, try to remember, and often he would, it was a much easier way to learn than from a book. They talked about work. It surprised Thomas, Raymond's interest in his job. Usually whenever people asked what he did and he replied, 'Bank manager,' they nodded and moved on to talk about something else, as if all the details and tasks of his working days were apparent to them from those two words. But Raymond seemed happy to listen, and it was a relief for Thomas, to be able to talk. Ann had stopped asking years before, and he knew she only half listened when he spoke about work, that she thought he was making a drama out of nothing much at all. But his job had changed; it was no longer the job he'd signed up to do, and it made him unhappy. The previous bank manager, and Thomas's own manager, Douglas Wright, had been the guardian of the bank's money, vetting and calculating risk, encouraging saving and urging caution, caution was the ethos of the bank back then. But by the time Douglas retired and Thomas was promoted to manager everything had changed. Thomas was tasked with meeting monthly lending targets, selling a certain number of loans every month, approving enough of the right type of mortgages. Thomas knew that Douglas had suffered sleepless nights after turning people down for mortgages, when there wasn't the money available to lend, but Thomas's sleeplessness was due to the pressure of selling. It seemed that the purpose of the bank had changed overnight, and with it Thomas's job. Thomas despised being a salesman. It wasn't in him. He cringed when he was browsing in a shop and a salesman approached him with a smile, and he hated to think that anyone would feel that way about him. But it had to be done; it was now his job to do it, and he tried, even though every instinct Thomas had was that of a careful, cautious banker, a banker from the old generation. And now he found himself working his way through his customer database, calling up those with a cushion in their account and suggesting ways to invest the money, or suggesting to less well-off customers they might want to take advantage of an introductory interest rate on a new credit card. Most people were polite, some were flattered to receive a phone call from their bank manager, others a little intimidated or nervous, and hardly anyone was ever rude, but Thomas still felt cheapened by it. Whenever he made one of these calls he instinctively leant his head into his right hand and rubbed his forehead until a red patch formed. The nadir for Thomas was an advert the bank ran. Posters all over the country of a bright red sports car, underneath the caption: *Why wait? Have it now!* It was the opposite of how Thomas had been raised, the opposite of how the bank had operated for years. What had happened to saving, sacrifice and patience? Where was the pleasure in a new car you couldn't afford, a car that would end up costing twice as much by the time it was paid off? Thomas told Ann about the advert, shaking his head as he did.

'What about this place?' Ann said.

'What about it?' Thomas asked.

'We needed the money for it, we didn't have it, my parents loaned us it. What's the difference?'

Thomas didn't argue, he couldn't bring himself to argue. If Ann couldn't see the difference what was the point?

Raymond was an easier confidant. He listened carefully and nodded at everything Thomas said. Whether he really agreed or not, Thomas couldn't tell and didn't mind much, it was good to get it out. In return Thomas encouraged Raymond to tell him about life on the farm, although the accounts Raymond haltingly relayed often amounted to nothing more than a list of the jobs he'd completed since they'd last walked together. But Thomas was keen to hear anyway, it was another world from his quiet, brown-carpeted, cream-walled bank. He was particularly interested in hearing about Chapman, the red-faced little man he'd met briefly once, in the gloomy farmhouse corridor, so he drew the tales out of Raymond.

'So you get ten minutes in the bathroom in the morning?'

'Any longer and you can hear him outside on the landing, shuffling and coughing.'

'What happens if you need longer?'

Raymond shrugged and said, 'I don't know, I stick to the ten minutes.'

'But they let you have your meals with them?'

'Sandwiches or soup at lunch and a hot meal at night. Sheila cooks.'

'So he feeds you at least?'

'He does, but it comes out of my pay. It's gone down a bit this year, because the price of food has gone up.'

If anyone other than Raymond had been speaking, Thomas would have suspected them of exaggerating for comic effect, but he doubted if Raymond had ever exaggerated anything in his life.

'Isn't it hard – living in the caravan? Can't you have a room in the house?'

'I'd rather stick with the caravan,' Raymond said, and Thomas laughed.

One night, after they'd been meeting and walking regularly for a few weeks, as they headed back to the road and Thomas's car, Thomas said, 'Do you fancy a pint one night? Over at the Tillotsons?'

Raymond said it would be nice.

'Thursday,' Thomas said, 'I'll pick you up.'

Later that night Raymond sat on the edge of his bed in the caravan trying not to fret, but fretting anyway.

Would he like a pint out? It was the question he'd been dreading, but the question he knew was inevitable; it was what men did – they went to the pub. Feelings of anxiety and stress immediately flooded his heart when Thomas made the suggestion – busy rooms, loud conversation, strangers looking; it was everything Raymond tried to avoid. But at least Thursday is soon, Raymond thought, at least there isn't too much time to worry and wait. Regardless, he did manage to cram a huge amount of worry into the next forty-eight hours. After tea on the Thursday, with his stomach feeling slick and greasy, Raymond asked if he could use the bathroom. 'Will there be any water?' he asked, hoping it didn't sound like a demand, worrying that Chapman would be annoyed by a second bathroom session of the day.

'There can be,' Sheila said. 'A date is it, Raymond?'

Raymond's cheeks flushed as if Sheila had pressed a button that released dye.

'Just going for a drink, he said, 'over at the Tillotsons.'

'With your new friend?' Sheila asked.

Raymond nodded.

'Well, good for you,' Sheila said, sounding a little peeved. 'He deserves a night out, doesn't he, Frank.'

Chapman didn't reply.

Back in the caravan, shiny and scrubbed, Raymond considered his clothes. But there wasn't too much to consider. He owned work clothes and evening clothes, which became work clothes over time. He pulled out his newest trousers and newest shirt, both of which were already years old, and his only pair of shoes. He was standing at the side of the road, waiting to be picked up ten minutes too early, thinking he really needed the toilet again, dreading the evening that lay in front of him. At one point he considered walking deep into the trees and hiding there until Thomas drove away, but he knew he wouldn't do that. A few seconds later he heard an engine approaching from behind the bend, and it was too late to escape.

When Thomas pushed the door of the Tillotsons open it was onto a packed little pub, groups of men standing together, holding pints, chatting, the faint thud of landing darts and the crack of pool balls coming from the snug. Thomas headed to the bar, smiling and nodding at people as he went, Raymond tracking right behind him. Raymond had wanted a deserted a pub; him and Thomas alone at a corner table, talking about the things they talked about on their walks, nobody noticing or staring. He kept his head down, wishing he was half his size, hating his huge body.

'What's your poison?' asked Thomas cheerfully, when they reached the bar.

'Bitter,' Raymond said, firmly. He knew that much. Men in Abbeystead drank bitter.

'Two pints of bitter then,' Thomas said and Raymond nodded. That was what you drank. That or mild.

As they turned with drinks in their hands, to head over to a table on the back wall, Raymond's cheeks burned red and his hands shook a little. Were people staring at him? Were they telling each other that it was Chapman's farmhand? The big man who never comes out, never says anything if he does? They finally reached a free table and sat down. Raymond felt hunted.

'Lively,' said Thomas.

Raymond agreed that it was, and because he didn't know what else to do, and because people went to the pub to drink, took a huge swig from the glass in front of him. He gulped down almost half the liquid in one go. He found it sweeter than he remembered, kinder to his tongue than he'd anticipated. He put the glass down and wiped his sleeve across his mouth.

Thomas laughed.

'That pint looks like a half in your hand,' he said, but he said it kindly, it didn't sting Raymond like a criticism. Raymond held his hands out, turned them over, considering them. 'People say they're big,' he said.

'I bet they're useful though,' said Thomas, 'with your work.'

'I suppose so,' agreed Raymond, 'but sewing buttons is tricky.'

Thomas laughed loudly, as if Raymond had made a joke, and Raymond joined in, pleased that the first thing he'd said in the pub had gone down well. He couldn't relax yet though, the next hurdle was coming up – he would have to negotiate the crowded room by himself, get to the bar, order more drinks, and somehow return them to the table unspilled. People would stare, they might try and talk to him, but he knew how important it was to buy the next drink. He'd learnt from Chapman that a man who accepted a drink and didn't buy the next one was not a man people liked to drink with. Seeing that Thomas was taking small sips, taking his time with his beer, Raymond let his pint sit on the table a while and waited until Thomas caught up.

They spoke about the usual things, which was a relief

to Raymond, at least the conversation didn't have to be different in the pub, but he couldn't concentrate as well as when they were out walking – the noise and the people swarming around them made it as difficult for Raymond as having a conversation in a heavy wind. He wasn't used to all the voices, mingling together, spilling into his ears, the sudden storms of laughter, the shouting of a name. Raymond watched Thomas carefully and tried to time his last gulp with Thomas's, and as soon as Thomas put his drained glass on the table Raymond grabbed it from him and headed to the bar, keen to get the ordeal over with. Raymond was served quickly and without any confusion and returned to the table without spilling the drinks on anyone. He sat down with a sigh. Thomas held up his drink and said, 'Cheers.' Raymond relaxed, just a little, for the first time that night. They ended up drinking four pints. Thomas usually stopped at three, he said, but Raymond wouldn't leave the pub owing a pint.

'You can get the first one next time,' Thomas had said, but Raymond was already up and off, on his second expedition to the bar.

Raymond climbed into his bed that night and slept more deeply than he'd slept for years. In the morning he couldn't remember, what, if anything, they'd spoken about on the way home. But he did remember he'd survived, and, in the end, enjoyed a night out at the pub. The next morning, mucking out, his head still a little woolly, Raymond stopped work suddenly. He stood straight-backed with fresh cow dung clumped thickly to the face of his shovel, his mouth open. 'Thomas is my friend,' was the thought he was thinking, the thought that had stunned him into stillness in the warm, shit-filled shippen.

Part Two

One

'You were right, Mum! Fast asleep!'

Harriet ran across the room and jumped into Thomas's lap. Thomas tickled her until she begged him to stop, until she nearly cried with it. Ann had taken the children to see her parents for the afternoon and now they were back they settled into their Sunday night routine. Daniel was upstairs playing computer games in his room, Harriet had been watching television alone but, as she often did, drifted to where Thomas and Ann were reading in the back room. She pulled one of her books from the shelves and lay down on her front on the floor, opened the book and furrowed her brow. The quiet was only broken by the rustle of Thomas's newspaper, Harriet's fidgeting feet and the occasional, thin music escaping Daniel's room. Thomas was half-reading a review of a film he had no intention of seeing when the knock came. He looked over to Ann, to see if she was expecting anyone, but Ann didn't glance up from her book and Harriet had already charged off. Thomas scanned the page for the last sentence he'd read and called out to Harriet. When he looked up the men were walking into the room. They stood against the wall, in a line, in front of a painting of sheep in the snow. Harriet was held by her shoulders.

'Where's your son?' the man holding Harriet asked.

Thomas's head was a thousand wasps. He couldn't think a thought.

Ann stood up and said, 'In his room. Upstairs.'

One of the men left the room.

Ann moved to follow but another man blocked the door.

'Is there anyone else in the house?' The first man again, the leader.

Ann shook her head.

'Are you expecting anyone tonight or in the morning?

Ann said, 'No,' and stepped forward towards Harriet, but the man's grip tightened and Harriet let out a whimper.

'Sit down,' he said. Ann walked backwards and sat on the edge of the chair, staring at the men with wild eyes.

'It's OK, Harriet, it's just a game,' she said, her voice sounding thin and stray. Thomas had lowered his paper but was still holding it, clinging until it nearly tore. His mouth hung open in a cartoon image of shock. The man returned with Daniel, and the leader, still with his hands on Harriet's shoulders, turned to Thomas and said, 'We will wait here until morning and then you will drive two of us to the bank. Two of us stay here with your wife and children. When they get a phone call that we're done the two remaining men will leave. Then you will be left in peace and you can ring the police. A few hours and it's over with.'

The wasps stopped for a second and Thomas spoke. 'I'm not leaving my family,' he said.

'You have no choice,' the man said. One hand left Harriet's shoulder, moved to his pocket and pressed down on something. The outline was clear. 'Everyone has one,' he said.

Thomas thought he might be sick.

'If we're at the bank at seven will anyone else turn up?' the man asked.

Thomas shook his head.

'What about cleaners?'

'They come at night.'

'No other members of staff?'

'Not until half eight.'

'Other than the alarm you turn off when we enter, what other alarms are there?'

'The counter is alarmed and the room where the safe is. They both have access codes.'

'And you know both of those?'

'Yes.'

'And the combination for the safe?'

'I'm the manager.'

'You'll be opening everything for us but I want you to write down all the codes anyway.'

He handed Thomas a pen and a slip of paper.

'What about panic buttons?'

'We don't have panic buttons.'

The man stared at Thomas. 'You don't have panic buttons?'

'Just the bigger branches.'

The man shook his head.

The children were allowed with their parents. Harriet rushed over and sat on Ann's knee, Daniel on Thomas's. Thomas noticed a sharp smell coming from Daniel and saw the damp patch spreading out from his crotch. 'It's OK,' he whispered in Daniel's ear, and held him tightly.

'Will you take your balaclavas off?' Ann asked. 'They're scaring the children.'

The leader shook his head. A minute later the man nearest the door, a short man, spoke. 'We aren't here to scare you. The masks just cover our faces, that's all.' The other men turned their heads to him and he fell silent.

At nine o'clock Ann addressed the leader and told him that the children would need to sleep. There was an anger in her voice, in her expression, Thomas wished she would lose. The leader told her that the children couldn't leave the room but Ann pestered until he sent two men to gather duvets and pillows from the children's rooms. When they returned Ann told them to go back for teddies and books. The two men looked to the leader, who nodded that they should do as they were told. This time Thomas asked for Daniel's pyjamas. The thought of these men touching his children's toys and clothes was a terrible one, but he wanted Daniel to be dry and comfortable. The short man swore as he left the room for a second time.

Thomas helped Daniel change behind the settee and Daniel whispered to Thomas that he needed the toilet again. When Thomas told the men, Harriet said to Ann that she needed to go too.

'One kid leaves the room accompanied by one of us,' the leader said, but Ann wouldn't agree to that. After discussion, two men, and Ann, accompanied the children one at a time to the downstairs toilet. Daniel went first. The men wouldn't allow the toilet door to be shut, so Ann stood in the doorway, blocking their view. They stayed close in case she tried to lock herself in the toilet with Daniel. When it was Harriet's turn she sat on the toilet, and after a few moments said, 'I can't go, Mummy, I can't go!' She quickly became hysterical and Ann moved forward to hug her, but the men pulled her back and Ann allowed herself to be dragged away. She wanted to hit and scratch, but that would only upset Harriet more. When it became clear Ann wasn't struggling the men released her and one of them rested his foot against the door so it couldn't be pulled shut, and Ann was allowed forward to Harriet. She held Harriet on the toilet and comforted her. Harriet continued to cry as they returned to the room. The short man patted her head and said, 'It'll be OK, love, this will soon be over with.' Ann slowed before she walked into the room and the man slowed instinctively with her. She leant down and whispered into his ear, 'Don't you fucking touch her.'

The men lined up against the wall, the children returned to their parents' laps.

'This isn't really a game, is it Mummy?' Harriet said.

'No, love,' Ann replied, resting her cheek on Harriet's head, 'it isn't.'

The short man stared at the two of them.

*

It was midnight but Raymond couldn't sleep. He decided to walk a few miles quickly, sometimes that was enough to encourage his body to accept tiredness. He entered the forest and headed north. He planned to walk a loop and be back at the caravan within an hour or so. Half an hour into the walk he spotted the white bonnet of a car on his right, parked underneath a tree, just off the side of a small track. He looked again and saw a smaller red car parked tightly behind it. He stopped to think and came to the only conclusion he could. A couple at it. The two girls from number 13 leapt into his mind, the grunting one, the shrieking one. 'We can hear you, you know . . . Grunt, grunt, grunt.' Raymond turned and walked quickly away. He was heading south now and came to the road which ran past Thomas's house. He decided to walk along the road, he could always step into the trees if he heard a car, and it was the quickest way back home. As he approached the house he could see a light from the kitchen. He'd never seen a light after midnight at the house and wondered if one of the children was sick. Or maybe someone can't sleep, like me, he thought. Maybe they're having a cup of tea, reading a book at the kitchen table, waiting for sleep to arrive. Insomnia wouldn't be too bad, if you were lucky to live in a house like that, Thomas believed. Knowing he wasn't the only person awake, even way out in the middle of Abbeystead, made him smile. He passed the house with a warm feeling for the family in his chest. He gave them a small wave as he went.

*

Thomas and Ann put Harriet and Daniel together on the couch and stayed with them until they did, eventually, unbelievably, fall asleep. Then they retreated to their chairs. 'You should try and sleep too,' the leader said to Thomas. 'We'll need you to be alert in the morning.' Thomas nearly laughed at the thought that he could sleep, but he caught himself. He didn't want to do anything that could be seen as provocative. These men had come into his house, they were holding his family hostage, and it was a kind of hell, he was sure of that, but there had been no violence up until now. What had happened so far could be recovered from, he believed. But if anyone was hurt, if Ann or the children were hurt, everything would change completely again. The men would consider him the main threat, so if he could show them he posed no threat at all, they wouldn't be on edge, they would be less likely to cause any damage. He glanced around the room and wondered if the house was ruined forever. As for sleep, the idea was ridiculous. My family is being held hostage in my own home, he thought. I was reading the newspaper on a Sunday night, and now there are men with guns in our house. He wanted to say that it didn't make sense, wonder how on earth it could happen, but it did make a horrible sense to him. All his adult life he'd lived with a sense of foreboding, the feeling that shadows were encroaching. When people were interviewed on television after a disaster or a brutal illness and said, with wide, astonished eyes, 'You just don't think it will ever happen to you,' Thomas had never understood. He always thought it might happen to him. It hadn't been a car crash for him, breast cancer for Ann, anything unspeakable happening to the children – instead it was four masked men on a Sunday night, standing against the wall of their lounge. And already he was realising the terror of it could not be contained in one dreadful night. He looked over at Daniel and Harriet and hoped they would sleep until it was all done with. If they could sleep through the night and he could get to the bank in the morning and get the men their money, it might not be something that would give them nightmares for years to come. Could it eventually be something they barely remembered? A hazy recollection he and Ann could diminish over the years, polish away with trips and treats and happy memories? Or would it be a dark seed in their heads, a seed that would grow until it filled their thoughts and affected everything they did?

What a terrible thing, not being able to protect your children.

Thomas jerked forward in his chair, causing the men to brace.

'What?' the leader said sharply, his hand moving to his pocket.

'Why don't we go now?' Thomas said, his voice ringing with hope. 'We could be there in half an hour. You could have the money and go. All of you.'

'No. We will leave in the morning. An hour before you normally leave.'

'Why?' asked Thomas, sounding as bewildered as a three-year-old who's been told to stop swinging mid-swing.

'We can't walk into a bank in the middle of the night,' the leader said.

Thomas spoke in a whine, his voice pleading. 'Nobody will be in Maltham after midnight. The pubs close at half ten, it's deserted by eleven. Empty.'

The leader didn't respond and Thomas shook his head, distraught that this would have to go on for hours yet.

The room had been silent for minutes when the short man spoke. He turned to the leader and said, 'You could go now. Then it's done.'

The leader walked over to the door and opened it. He gestured sharply for the man to leave the room and followed him out, closing the door behind him. A short burst of words could be heard, followed by a cry of pain. Seconds later the door opened and the short man shuffled back into the room, gasping for breath, gripping his stomach, the leader walking slowly behind him. The man walked over to the wall and bent himself double, rubbing his stomach. Eventually he looked up. Thomas saw the man look directly at Ann. Ann was straight-backed in her chair and returned the look with cold clarity until the man dropped his head and gripped his stomach again. Thomas was shaking. Violence was in the house.

At five o'clock Thomas did fall asleep for twenty exhausting minutes. As soon as his eyes opened he turned to check on Ann and the children. Everyone was where they had been. Everyone was asleep. The men were still over by the wall. As dawn broke and light spread into the room Thomas realised that daylight didn't make anything better. The only comfort he could take was that it was no longer eight, or ten o'clock the previous night. It was no longer the pitch-black desperate hour of one in the morning. Soon he would be able to get the men their money and, if they were telling the truth, get rid of them.

At six the leader ordered Thomas to get up. He and another man accompanied Thomas upstairs and watched him change. Thomas pulled on trousers, a shirt, jacket and shoes and turned to the men.

'A tie,' the leader said.

'What?'

'You normally wear a tie?'

Thomas nodded that he did.

'Well put one on.'

As Thomas groped in the dark of his wardrobe he felt a dot, a particle, of respect for the man.

At six thirty they went. The children woke at the movement and noise in the room and immediately began to cry. Thomas walked over to kiss them goodbye, but he was pulled away and pushed towards the door. It was the first time he'd been touched by the men. They were tense now, and tired. There was a strain in their movements.

The leader spoke to the two men staying behind.

'Sit with them,' he said to the men. 'Keep them in this room, they can't leave this room. That is your job.'

To Ann and the children he said, 'And all you have to do is wait, and then your dad will come home.'

He walked Thomas away. As Thomas left through the front door he could hear his children crying behind him, Ann doing her best to comfort them. But they weren't crying tears of frustration, unfairness, or a scraped knee. They were terrified tears and it hurt him to hear them. Then he was driving to work, a man with a gun lying on the back seat of his car. Another car appeared behind him as he left the forest. Thomas looked in his mirror but the car stayed too far back and he couldn't see who was driving or make out anything about the car other than it was white.

'Eyes forward,' said a voice coming from the prone body in the back of the car.

*

Harriet and Daniel buried themselves into their mother, sobbing. Ann held them as tightly as she could. The two men stood against the wall, as if they would never leave. It was the short man and a man who hadn't said a word all night who remained. When the children had calmed a little the silent man spoke, his voice sounding like it had been buried in sand.

'Your phone should ring in about an hour. I will answer it and then we will leave. You need to wait half an hour before phoning the police.'

'You're asking me to wait?' Ann said.

'If we meet any police on these roads we will know you rang them early. If you wait half an hour there will be no recriminations for anyone. It's safer and better for us all.'

'What will happen to my husband?'

'He'll be left at the bank. Safe. Everyone will be fine.'

'Do you think the children will be fine?'

The man remained silent.

'People like you,' Ann said. 'You're worse than dogs.'

*

The phone rang. The man left to answer. He was gone only seconds before reappearing at the door. 'Let's go,' he said, and turned away. The short man walked forward, pulled his fist back and punched Ann as hard as he could, striking her in the left eye. The children screamed and grabbed at Ann. Ann pushed them away quickly and roughly, leaving them as staggered as they were distressed, but she needed all her strength to hold her head together because it was breaking apart. Splintered cheekbones were falling from her face, falling through her fingers. Her skull was collapsing. When she could, with her hands still covering her face, she looked up. The men were gone. Ann slowly removed her hands, expecting a mess to drop to the floor in front of her, but somehow shattered bones didn't fall. She walked to the front door, locked it and checked the back door was locked too. Then she stood at the kitchen sink, rallying herself, knowing she needed to touch her face, to wipe the blood away at least. Finally she wet a cloth and dabbed as delicately as she could around her eye. Already the skin surrounding the eye socket was ballooning out; threatening to burst open like a climactic firework. She held onto the sink. The floor underneath her rolled and swirled like a drunk man dancing.

Thirty minutes passed and then, with the children still crying and holding onto her, Ann picked up the phone and dialled. She explained as best she could what had happened, but the voice asked too many questions. Ann interrupted part way through the third question, repeated the address and hung up. She remained stood by the phone, the children standing behind her. Ann was an atheist and wouldn't pray for Thomas, how cowardly that would be, but she dropped to her knees, lowered her head and closed her eyes. It was the only thing she could think to do. She didn't appeal to a higher being, she didn't ask for Thomas to be returned to her unharmed, she simply thought of him. Daniel and Harriet looked at their kneeling mum and then, Daniel first, lowered themselves to the floor, closed their hands and closed their eyes. The children did pray. The three of them, in the hallway, kneeling in a row.

Two

On Tuesday night Raymond waited for Thomas, but when Thomas didn't appear he set off for the walk by himself. When Thomas didn't turn up for the Thursday night drink Raymond wondered if the family had gone away on holiday and Thomas had forgotten to tell him, but that didn't seem like Thomas. Raymond then worried whether he'd said or done something to upset Thomas and he racked his brains but couldn't come up with anything. It wasn't until Friday night, over tea, when he learnt what had happened.

'You don't know?' Sheila said, her eyes sparkling, excitement moving through her. 'They were held hostage. Your mate, the whole family. And then they drove him off in the morning and robbed his bank.'

'How much did they get?' asked Chapman.

'I don't know. Thousands. Thousands. They tied them up – even the little ones – tied them up together. Had them there all weekend. Imagine it.'

'He'd have been better if he'd stayed in town. Somebody would have noticed something going on then,' said Chapman, shovelling a chunk of sausage into his mouth.

Raymond had stopped eating. He must have been staring at Sheila because she looked annoyed and said, 'It's true, Raymond. Every last word.'

Raymond didn't know what to say. It was everything he dreaded about the world all at once.

Back in the caravan, distressed, Raymond's mood plummeted further when he realised he'd walked past the house on the Sunday night. He remembered the lights being on late, and then he remembered the two cars, parked bumper to bumper, the red and the white car, hidden under the trees. He'd thought they were the cars of lovers but the cars must have belonged to the men. He became agitated. The cars and the light. Shouldn't he have worked it out? The caravan couldn't contain Raymond and his agonising and soon he was out, striding up the road. He didn't bother with the fields or the forest, he didn't care about being spotted, he could walk harder and faster on the tarmac, and he needed to walk quickly. Half an hour later he was approaching the house and even from a distance he could see changes. There was an alarm box fitted above the door, a camera on the front corner of the house, pointing to the road. Raymond believed Sheila then, or at least believed some trouble had occurred. Sheila liked a story, she was known for her wild tales, her exaggerations, and until Raymond saw the evidence at the house he was clinging to the hope that she'd outdone herself with her latest gossiping. He paused at the door, unsure if he was going to knock, he'd never called at the house before, but he was knocking at the door before he'd realised he'd made a decision. Understanding the house would be on high alert Raymond stood back from the door, where he could easily be seen. He looked up and saw Thomas at an upstairs window, peering down. Raymond lifted a hand to wave and Thomas waved back and disappeared, but the front door remained closed.

Three

They met the day of the job, Keith and John, in the Victoria. They agreed to be there at three, after catching up on sleep, but neither man found sleep easy to come by. Keith turned up at two and John was not far behind. When he returned home that morning Keith had hidden the money, more money than he'd ever possessed, in the corner of the attic, underneath junk that hadn't been moved for years, junk that had been left by previous tenants. Then he'd eaten and gone to bed, where sleep evaded him. Walking through town Keith was frustrated – he should have been happy but he felt angry and dislocated. It was lack of sleep, he told himself, as he entered the pub, the comedown after a big night.

It was a quiet afternoon at the pub and he found a table in the corner of an empty room and huddled down with his drink. John arrived shortly and they drank for a while, discussing the likelihood of getting caught, of getting away with it. And then Keith asked the question he'd been desperate to ask, the question he'd been wondering about since he'd counted his money.

'How much did you get?'

John paused and then said, 'Twenty. You?'

Keith relaxed and nodded. 'Same, twenty.'

He was concerned he would receive less because he was the last one to join the group, the last one to be involved, and he knew the leader had never liked him.

'How much do you think they took?' he asked John.

'More. But they earned it.'

'Just because they went to the bank? It doesn't seem fair.'

John sighed. 'You know why they took more, Keith, I've told you. They spent months on this. They watched banks all over the place, followed people home, checked out the security arrangements. And when they'd chosen the bank and the worker, they watched the house. Stood in that forest for hours, made sure they knew the family's routine, so there would be no surprises. And there weren't any surprises, were there.'

Keith nodded. 'Still, I wonder how much they took if they gave us that much.'

'Just be pleased you got what you did and it all went well.'

Keith didn't like the tone of John's voice. He put it down to tiredness.

'You really don't know who they are?' he asked.

'I met them a few weeks ago. Someone recommended me to them. They never told me their names and told me not to ask. I know they aren't from round here, that's all. The price for me being involved was that I had to find one other person for the job, and I found you.'

'And they didn't pay you for finding me?'

'No. And you were lucky, you didn't have to do anything other than turn up.'

'It was about time. I was owed some luck.'

Keith looked over to the bar and the landlord, a fat man in his sixties reading the paper, smoking a roll-up, drinking a pint, his face red and shiny, a chip butty on a plate next to him. Can't be much time left for him, Keith thought. He hoped the pub wouldn't change when he was gone; he liked the place with its old carpet, small cramped rooms and cheap beer. Maybe he could be a landlord, he thought, with all the money he owned now, an investment. Keith drank some of his pint and laughed at himself, dismissing the idea. Why would he want to work after he'd seen how easy it was to get his hands on £20,000? He looked at John.

'But now we know where to go in the future. What's to stop us doing something similar when we need more money? It didn't need four of us. We could do it, me and you.'

John swirled the beer at the bottom of his glass. 'You shouldn't have hit her,' he said.

Keith shrugged. He'd been waiting for that. And he'd been wondering if hitting the woman so brutally was the reason he felt flat, out of focus, but he didn't think it could be. He'd hit women before without feeling like this. Women he liked, women he regretted having to hit. And this one deserved it. The man, he'd been shitting himself, but after the woman had pulled herself together, after the original shock, she'd been almost dismissive of them. Demanding things for the children, saying what she would and wouldn't allow to happen. 'Don't you fucking touch her,' she'd said to Keith when he'd been nice to the little girl. When he'd been nice to her! And she didn't say it as if she was worried about him being a kiddy fiddler. It was more like she believed a man like him wasn't suited to deal with a child like hers. Regardless of the fact that she was a prisoner in her own home, that the family were at their mercy, she acted above it all.

As if the men were an irritant. Keith had wished he did have a gun on him. He would have loved to have pulled it out, pointed it, waved it at the children, and seen how superior she was then. Seen how much of an irritant he was then.

Keith picked up his pint and said, 'I didn't like her, that was all.'

John shook his head. 'You still shouldn't have hit her. Not like that.'

Keith suppressed the anger he felt. He didn't want to fall out with John, not today.

'Forget it,' he said, taking a drink from his pint. 'It all worked out, didn't it.' He pushed his glass forward and John met it, and they quietly toasted their success.

It was the first of many drinks. John left the pub at six craving food and sleep, but Keith carried on celebrating. After a few pints his mood settled and he couldn't stop thinking about the money in the attic, the money in his pocket. He started to smile. He filled the jukebox with coins, he took requests. He wanted to drag every second of enjoyment out of the day and pull it towards him. Keith finally left the pub after last orders had been called and the towels draped over the pumps. It was only a twenty-minute walk back to his house, but it took him nearly an hour. Lamppost to lamppost. Sometimes falling over, nearly always singing or shouting. As he finally reached the front door of 13 Granville Road he punched the air twice and fumbled for his key. Who said Keith Sullivan would never come to any good? Who fucking said that?

Four

'There was nothing you could have done.'

Thomas pulled his hand away from his coffee cup. 'What do you mean?'

'Exactly that. There was nothing you could have done.'

Ann tried to take Thomas's hand but he pulled away from her too. Anger scattered across the inside of his head.

'Did you want me to wrestle them?' he asked. 'Did you want me to take them on one by one?'

'Thomas, don't,' Ann said. 'All we could do was sit there and do nothing.'

'Nothing? Is that what you thought I was doing?'

How could she look at him through her battered eye and say that? Could she not see what he had been doing? The position he'd been put in? How every possible action had been taken away from him until he was a man locked in a cell, chained to a wall. But still, even in those circumstances, he'd done everything within his power to keep his family safe. She had to see that. Thomas looked across the table at Ann. At the hideous purple and blue eye settled like a crater in the white pale of the rest of her skin. Did she really think he'd done nothing? Could she not see a lesser man would have argued, grandstanded? Thomas had lost every inch of pride and honour sat in that chair in front of his family, every course of action disabled to him. But he'd done all he could. He'd put on a fucking tie! The only thought in his head for twelve hours was to protect his family, and his wife thought he'd done nothing. How he wished he'd come home to a burglar climbing through the window, a man he could have challenged, a man he could have fought. Or if he'd seen a man on the street, threatening a woman. A drunk husband, shaved head, fat arms, pulling the woman's hair, taking a kick at her. Thomas wouldn't walk away from that. But to put a man in the position where the safest thing he can do for his family is to sit in a chair and wait and hope is cruel. To have his children wide-eyed and shaking, wetting themselves . . .

Ann had been angry. Her anger had put them all at risk. Four men in their house with guns and his wife was angry at the violation, making demands, trying to claw back ground. He wasn't surprised when he came home to be confronted by her claggy black eye. He wasn't surprised, but he still burst into tears.

'Not in front of the children,' Ann had said, ushering him into their bedroom and closing the door, where he'd sat on the bed and sobbed. She told him that the short man, the loose cannon, had simply walked forward and punched her in the face, just as they left. She had no idea why. Thomas didn't believe her. As much as his legs went weak and his heart broke when he saw his wife's battered face, he didn't believe she'd done nothing to provoke the punch that landed with such force on her eye. He'd flinched at the anger she'd shown the men, prayed that she would remain calm and stop the demands and requests. But throughout the night she'd needled and nagged them. How could she not see that they weren't dealing in rights and wrongs? Men with guns in your house take what they want, and all you can do is hope that they don't take everything.

'There was nothing you could have done.'

He'd done everything in his power.

The night after it happened, putting the children to bed, a police car at the front of the house, Harriet voiced the question that clanged like a town-hall bell inside Thomas's head.

'What if they come back?' she asked, clutching her favourite teddy to her chest.

'They won't come back, sweetheart,' Ann said, tucking Harriet in tightly.

'Really? They won't come back?'

'Of course not. They wouldn't be that stupid.'

Downstairs a pacing and incredulous Thomas said, 'How can you say that to her? That the men won't come back. They might come back.'

'Shall I tell our eight-year-old daughter that, Thomas?' Ann asked. 'That she should never fall asleep feeling safe in her own house? They don't win. We can either decide that now, or drive ourselves mad with it.'

Thomas didn't know where strength like that came from. He only knew his hands were shaking and he was listening, every second, for the sound of a car, the fall of a footstep, the crack of a twig.

Five

Keith had given Rose £300 and the girls £100 each in the days following the job. The girls had leapt on the money, waved it in the air, kissed the notes and screamed, had even kissed Keith. Rose took the money but her acceptance wasn't joyful or without question. Despite her questioning all Keith would tell her was that the money was a thank you for putting up with him through the hard times. In the following weeks, whenever money was needed for bills or food, Rose would tell Keith it was time he was back out looking for work and cash would quickly be handed over. Keith showed no sign of looking for a job, was sleeping even later than usual, drinking every night. Rose understood the money hadn't come to Keith through any honest endeavour, but she took it. It was a fraction of what he owed her, she believed. She bought a dress and a pair of shoes from the £300 and put the rest in an account Keith didn't know existed. Each time he was generous with cash she paid as much as she could afford into the account and, despite the seemingly never-ending stream of money from Keith, would walk the extra half-mile to the cheaper shops as usual.

Keith wasn't interested in saving money. He bought a new wardrobe of clothes and a woman in town was kept busy raising hems and shortening legs until each new item fitted Keith with the precision he sought. He bought himself a car, a second-hand red Ford Escort, and taxed and insured it. He went out every night. His decision to spend the money freely was a considered one. He realised he could live off the money longer if he lived carefully and soberly, but that approach didn't appeal to Keith. There was a man who drank in the Victoria a couple of times a week. He ordered half a pint of the cheapest beer and counted out his money to the exact amount from a plastic coin bag. He noticed when the prices went up by a penny and reacted like the barman was holding a gun to his head when he held out his hand for the money. This man knew which supermarkets marked their prices down when, which butcher would sell meat cheaply and would sit at the bar crowing about saving £2 on a nasty cut of meat you wouldn't feed a dog. Keith despised him. The sight of the man in his ugly shoes and thin coat depressed Keith to his core. The delight he took in saving a few pence on a nearly stale loaf of bread mystified Keith. If that was living, Keith would rather be dead. He'd even tried to buy the man a drink once, just to cheer himself up, so he didn't have to sit and watch a middle-aged man in market-bought clothes slowly sipping at half a pint, but the miserable sod wouldn't accept it. 'Thank you but no,' he'd said firmly, holding a hand over his glass as if Keith might be about to pour the drink by some form of magic, 'I drink what I can afford.' There was a prissy smugness to the man that enraged Keith. It was as if he enjoyed the dismal constraints of his life. Keith's decision to live life the opposite way to this man was a conscious one. If he wanted it, he had it. Money went on taxis, meals out, the horses and drinking. And, of course, clothes. Walking past Green's one day he saw Eric Calpin, his boss from the cement works, trying on a jumper, a dumpy woman at his side. Keith's eyes were immediately drawn to a leather jacket in the window. He sought out the price tag quickly. £150. That was enough. Keith walked into the shop, interrupted the young shop assistant who was handing another jumper to Eric and pointed to the window and said, 'How much for the jacket?'

The assistant glanced to the window and said, 'I'd have to check. A hundred and fifty I think.'

'I'll take it,' said Keith, clapping his hands together.

The assistant looked at the small man in front of her. 'We have different sizes if that one doesn't fit,' she said.

'It's fine, I'll take it.' Keith's cheeks smarted a little.

The assistant apologised to Keith's ex-boss, walked over to the window, took the jacket from the mannequin and carried it to the till.

'Why not try it on?' she said, holding the large jacket up in the air, a plea in her voice. 'It'll only take a second.'

'Just put it in the bloody bag,' Keith said quietly, staring at the girl.

The assistant, red-cheeked herself now, carefully folded the jacket and said, as coldly as she could whilst asking for such a large amount of money, 'A hundred and fifty pounds please.'

Keith looked at the man who'd sacked him, pulled out a roll of notes, slowly counted out the money and handed it over. Keith left the shop with a jacket he didn't particularly care for, a jacket that certainly didn't fit, happiness dancing in his legs, joy wriggling in his chest. He crossed the road to the nearest pub, climbed on a bar stool and said, 'Enjoy your polyester jumper and your fat wife, you fat bastard.' He grinned broadly at the approaching barman.

Through drink Keith managed to hold melancholy at bay until the end of the night most days. The words that depressed him, the words he dreaded to hear were, 'Time, ladies and gentlemen. Glasses please.' It was then the sadness would catch up with him, another day gone, no more excitement or fun to be found, everyone off home to bed. At first, with the pile of cash thick and weighty, Keith managed to smile, even after last orders; he knew he could do it all again the next day and the day after that. For a while Keith was as happy as he'd ever been. Money in his pocket provided all the joy he ever thought it could.

There were three downsides to his new life that caused Keith pain. Firstly, and a daily problem, were the hangovers. His drinking started earlier and finished later as the weeks progressed and he spent most mornings recovering in bed, sweating in the sheets, praying that he would soon feel better, vowing to take it easier that night. Secondly, and a direct result of the drink again, he was gaining weight. The fat seemed to appear from nowhere; for years he'd been drinking and eating at will, with no obvious effect and then, suddenly, a pot belly was heavy at his front. For the first time in his life Keith was forced to buy a bigger trouser size.

'You need to watch the weight,' Rose said. 'A short man like you can easily start to look like a ball.'

Keith was dumbfounded. Rose had never once referred to his height in all their years together.

The belly was bad enough but to Keith's horror it wasn't only his midriff that was collecting the fat, it was attacking his face too. When he caught sight of himself in the bathroom mirror he could see the extra flesh had spread to his cheeks and neck. Jowly, was the word. His once handsome face was turning into a pale, paunchy mess.

Finally, and by far the biggest worry, was the money. As satisfyingly large as the amount had been in the beginning, every day it grew relentlessly smaller. And as the money shrank, his future shrank with it and resentment began to seep back into his heart. Even before he was halfway through the money he was starting to fret. His mood would turn ugly quickly and the girls knew to stay out of his way and Rose became wary again, watching what she said and monitoring Keith's arms and legs for any sign of a threat. The nights in the pubs banished his worry underneath drink for a few hours, but the mornings brought the hangover hand in hand with the dismal realisation that one day his money would run out.

Six

Thomas and Ann met Dr Barbour in a pale green room at the back of the health centre in Maltham. The doctor spoke in a low, controlled voice and poured them water from a jug with a steady hand. They were there to discuss the children, the possible consequences of the night. When they were introduced and settled, Dr Barbour crossed her legs and said, 'I have an understanding of what happened from our initial conversation, but why don't we begin by you talking me through it, from the start?' Thomas wondered whether she was supposed to cross her legs. He remembered a course work had sent him on a couple of years before. Crossed legs conveyed defensiveness and hostility, didn't they? Or maybe that was just crossed arms, he couldn't quite remember. By the time he'd considered this Ann had begun to retell the facts of the night. She spoke plainly, without emotion or drama. The more she spoke the more anxious Thomas grew. She wasn't conveying the true horror of it all. At one point he interrupted and said, 'They had guns.'

'They said they had guns,' Ann told the woman. 'We didn't actually see them.'

'You could see them,' Thomas said. 'You could see the outline.'

When Ann was coming to the end of her account, without mentioning the violence, he jumped in again. 'They hit Ann, in front of the children. Right in the face.' He held his hand over his eye to show where his wife had been attacked.

Dr Barbour listened carefully throughout, nodding and encouraging Ann to continue with her account, welcoming Thomas's interruptions when he made them. Thomas was surprised she didn't make notes.

When Ann finished Dr Barbour uncrossed her legs and started to speak. Her advice was simple common sense – thinking they would have arrived at themselves, but hearing a professional speaking, in her steady and smooth voice, was soothing and reassuring and Thomas and Ann were happy to listen.

'Talk to your children about what happened,' she said. 'Don't gloss over it, get it out there, something you talk about as a family. Things fester and grow if they are kept in the dark, if they are not spoken about. Talk to them about what the men did, why they did it, and why it was wrong. Tell them that adults don't always behave as they should, that they sometimes do bad things and have to be punished, just like children. Ask them if they were scared, if they are still scared now.'

'What do we say if they want to know if we were scared?' Ann asked. A question from his wife that surprised Thomas.

'You tell them the truth. It's a shock to children to find out that their parents aren't invincible. It might be a lesson they learn sooner than their school friends, but it won't hurt them. It's important to reassure them too. Tell them how rarely something like this happens. How have they been? Tell me how they've reacted since it happened.'

'Harriet has wet the bed a few times,' Ann said, 'and Daniel has nightmares that have made him frightened to go to sleep.'

Dr Barbour nodded. 'These are natural reactions to what has happened,' she said. 'You should tell them that, and let them know that there is nothing wrong with how they are feeling. Their bodies are processing stress, that's all.'

'What do we say if they ask if it will happen again?' Thomas asked. That was the question he needed the answer to, and not just for the children. He turned down the television so he could listen for any noise and at night, in bed, he strained his ears for the slightest twinge of sound.

'You've increased security?' Dr Barbour asked.

'A camera and an alarm,' Thomas said.

'Well, point that out to them,' she said. 'Tell them the changes that have been made, explain how they make you safer, and statistically it's very unlikely that something like this will ever happen to you again. You can tell them that as the truth.'

'And we've told them not to answer the door,' Thomas said.

Dr Barbour smiled at Thomas. 'I would suggest you urge your children to show caution, but you don't want them afraid of a knock at the door.'

'But that's how they got in.'

'Still, how many times have you had a knock at the door in your life and it was someone meaning to cause you harm?'

'I understand that, but all it needs is for it to be that one time.'

'But if you apply that approach logically, that every person you don't know is a potential threat, you will never leave the house again, never let anyone into your house.'

Thomas scratched his face. 'Logic tends to go out of the window after something like this,' he said.

'It's natural to feel like that. But my point is that reasoned thinking can help redress the balance, can help you get back to some sort of normality and, eventually, peace. Catastrophes happen very rarely. You get up, live your life and go to bed on the vast majority of days. You don't want to spend the rest of your life guarding against something that might never materialise.'

'But it's already materialised.'

'And statistically, it is very unlikely to materialise again.'

'But you hear, don't you, on the news. Burglars go back to houses they've burgled before. They wait until new items are bought on insurance and they clear it out again. Why shouldn't the same thing happen to us? They got away with a hell of a lot of money very easily. Why wouldn't they try it again? Or another lot? They hear about it and want a go too?' Thomas had become agitated. His voice was raised, he was sitting forward in his chair.

'It's natural to have these fears,' Dr Barbour said. 'And fear can be a good thing. It means we don't walk too close to the cliff edge, we don't drive too fast on a wet road. And already it has made you take action;

you've increased security. But if you give fear too much rein it goes from being useful to controlling. I understand you are worried about what happened to you and your family happening again, of course you are, but you don't want it to control your life from now on. You don't want to live life with the constant belief that something terrible is about to happen.'

'Lightning doesn't strike twice,' said Thomas.

'It does, actually. Just rarely. That's my point.'

The room fell quiet. Ann allowed the quiet to settle and then spoke.

'Should the children come and see you?'

'I will leave that up to you. I'm happy to see them but you know your children better than anyone. Talk to them and see what you think. Any worries, any concerns, bring them to me. Everyone is different, children too. One child might brush something like this off reasonably easily, whilst another will be hugely affected, sometimes for a long time. Keep an eye on them and keep in touch with me. Believe it or not your children are very lucky. This is a hard thing to happen to a family, but you clearly love your children and want to support them. I can't always say that about everyone I see.'

Thomas was surprised to hear the word 'love' come from the mouth of the woman, surprised to hear it spoken in such an ugly room. But when you got down to the bare bones of it, when you considered everything, that was what it came down to. That simple, short, soft word. It didn't sound anything like it felt to Thomas right then.

'She made a lot of sense,' Ann said on the drive home.

Thomas didn't reply. He wasn't sure that she had made much sense at all. Words spoken in a safe room were nothing. He wanted a steel wall around the house. He wanted men in watchtowers, with guns.

Seven

Raymond lay on the bed in the caravan, staring up at the same cracks and scuffs in the roof he'd stared at for years. He hadn't seen Thomas for weeks and wasn't sure if he would ever see him again. It was a new type of sadness that was holding him and Raymond had only just realised that it was probably loneliness. And now, looking back, it surprised him how easily he'd grown accustomed to friendship, how quickly he'd embraced it after years of guarding himself against the world of people. But Tuesday and Thursday nights had given him contact with the world, rescued him from the miserable mutterings of Chapman for a while, stolen him away from his own predictable thoughts and worryings. Raymond had visited Thomas's house twice again, knocking at the door and standing back in the road both times, but nobody answered the door and Raymond didn't think he could go to the house and knock for a third time.

*

Thomas had been an easy man to talk to but at first Raymond played safe and kept the burden of conversation away from himself by asking Thomas questions. He'd even thought up questions beforehand, in case Thomas ran out of things to say and the focus turned on him. But as the weeks passed and Raymond began to relax in Thomas's company he found himself talking about the farm and the house in Etherton, his jobs on the sites in the early days and, eventually, his mother. He was shocked when he found himself describing her last months. He told Thomas things he didn't usually allow himself to think about.

'They would get her into a chair during the day when they could, and she would sit there with her head down, and then suddenly she would scream, "I'm falling! I'm falling!" and you would try and hold her hand and tell her she was alright, she was safe, she wasn't falling, but it wouldn't make any difference.'

Raymond told Thomas about one of the most upsetting incidents, something he'd never told anyone. It happened when his mother was still living at home. He'd left her alone in the morning to go to work, but she'd let herself out of the house, still in her dressing gown, and set off down the street, heading towards town. At the level crossing her walking stick had jammed into the rail line and in her attempts to pull it free she fell over. People tried to help but she was lying on the track, bleeding from her head, still gripping the walking stick, refusing to let go, and a train was due. The police and an ambulance were called, the train was delayed and his mother was taken to hospital. Word got to Raymond and he rushed to be with her. He found her asleep in a small room by herself and sat down on a chair in the corner. Eventually a doctor came in. 'She's confused,' the doctor told Raymond. 'Don't be alarmed when she wakes.' Raymond dozed off himself, waking at clattering in the corridor. When he looked over to his mother he could see she was awake too and staring back at him. It was early evening and in the half-light of the hospital room her eyes looked like black pennies.

'I never liked you,' she said. 'Never trust that one, I thought, the second I saw you. Never liked you one bit.' Her weak voice shook as she spoke and she didn't take her eyes off him.

'It's me, Mother,' he said, 'Raymond.'

He stood up, to prove himself, to move closer, to reassure her that she was mistaken, but as soon as he rose from the chair she screamed like the devil was coming for her. A nurse rushed in and shooed Raymond out of the room.

'I see this a lot,' the nurse said to Raymond, later. 'When they are as confused as this they often turn on loved ones. It's the cruellest thing, but you mustn't let it upset you. It's not you she's talking to and it's not really her any more saying the words.'

Raymond said he understood and thanked the nurse, but he couldn't forget the words and the fierce glare of the dark eyes. They'd always been so close, he thought they'd always been so close. Could the illness be dragging the truth out of her the way drink sometimes did with drunks? Raymond didn't think so, most of the time he didn't think so, but in his darkest hours he wondered.

After Raymond finished Thomas was silent for a while and then he stopped walking and said, 'That must have been awful.'

Raymond nodded his head. It had been awful. The last few months of her life, every day was awful in some way.

On a Thursday night, weeks after he'd waved at Thomas in the upstairs window, Raymond found himself stood outside the Tillotsons. The door was open wide and he could hear the chatter from inside and smell the cigarettes and beer. Raymond shifted on his feet and stared at the pub. He couldn't pretend that he'd been on a walk and just happened to end up at the village – after his tea he'd washed and changed into his good clothes and followed the roads directly to where he was now stood. He hadn't allowed himself to think too much about what he was doing, letting instinct take over, but when he found himself outside the pub he realised he couldn't go in. It was impossible. He listened to the noise for a few more seconds and then turned and headed away up the road, back to the covering trees.

Eight

Ann spoke to the children. She took them for a walk along the river and asked them questions about the night. Harriet held her hand and called the intruders 'the bad men', and said it in a scolding voice, as if they had stolen an apple each. She told Ann she thought the security camera was a good idea.

'Not if they wear masks again. What's the point in it then?' Daniel said, and tried to trip his sister up. Daniel spent most of his time looking for stones and sticks to throw into the river, moaning about having to be on the walk. He answered Ann's questions bluntly, seemingly annoyed at having to talk at all. Ann remembered the nights when he'd come crying to her and Thomas, shaking and shocked from nightmares of the men. He'd snuggled between the two of them and she'd held him until he felt safe enough to sleep again. He'd spent less time in his bedroom, had sat with her in the kitchen, followed her to the lounge, not wanting to be alone. Ann felt a swathe of guilt when she realised she missed scared Daniel. Recently he was back to being surly, irritated by her mere presence. If he was traumatised he was doing a good job of convincing her otherwise. Harriet had stopped wetting the bed and was back to talking about what she'd done at school, who her new best friend was, why she loved Mrs Chatburn, all the things she used to chatter about. Ann had found her checking that the front door was locked a few times and Daniel would appear from his room if Thomas was more than five minutes late, but that behaviour was to be expected, wasn't it? Just a natural reaction.

Ann felt conflicted.

She didn't want the children to have to talk about the night endlessly; if they were doing well, why drag it up over and over? But she didn't want to neglect them either. She didn't want them as angry teens screaming at her about how they were never given the chance to talk, how their uncaring parents had brushed it all under the carpet. She wondered if they spoke to one another about the night. There was a two-year gap between them and they shared no real interests, but Daniel could be surprisingly tender and patient with Harriet at times. Ann could barely bring herself to acknowledge the feeling, but sometimes, yes, she felt jealous of the tenderness he showed his sister. A couple of weeks ago Ann had found them in Daniel's room, sat on opposite sides of his bed and she'd obviously walked in on something, they were quickly silent and Harriet was hardly ever allowed in Daniel's room. 'Everything OK?' Ann asked, and they both nodded and stayed quiet, chatty Harriet suddenly as tight-lipped as her brother. Ann left them to it. No, that wasn't true, she closed the door and lingered on the landing, but they carried on their conversation in tiny whispers and Ann couldn't make out a word. But if they were talking to each other about the night, that was a good sign, wasn't it? A sign of a healthy family. Eventually, towards the end of the walk, when the loop was almost complete and the car was in sight, she asked the children if they wanted to talk to someone, a special type of doctor, about what had happened the night the men came. Harriet seemed bewildered by the offer, almost upset. Daniel was reliably dismissive. Ann decided then. Parental instinct. They would scream at her when they were teenagers anyway. She took both of them by their shoulders and pulled them to her, one on either side. Surprisingly Daniel allowed it, and they walked together for a minute before Daniel spotted a pile of sheep droppings and broke away to kick them as hard as he could into the river.

Thomas was more of a problem. He was a mess. His face had changed, Ann was sure of it. The forehead was lower, the eyes narrower, you could see the stress etched into his scowls, the weight on his brow. He had no patience with the children, couldn't stand noisy games or shouting. The television had to be turned to a whisper, the radio was snapped off when he walked in the room. They hadn't made love since it had happened. He came home one day and found an album playing, the volume high, drum machines and keyboards filling the house. He strode over to the stereo and pulled the needle from the vinyl just as Ann walked back into the room.

'What are you doing?' he asked her, sounding bewildered.

'Listening to one of my old albums,' Ann said.

'Why?'

They stared at each other across the room.

'You have to stop this,' Ann said. 'It's not good for the children, you behaving this way.'

Thomas shook his head. 'I'm doing my best.'

'It's not enough.'

‘I don’t know how you can carry on like this.’ Thomas gestured towards the stereo.

‘We’ve spoken about this, Thomas. Life has to continue. Fearing them is letting them win. And it’s a bad environment for the children.’

‘I don’t know how to feel any differently,’ Thomas said.

‘You need to try.’ Ann tried to speak more kindly. ‘Have you thought about seeing someone? We could make you an appointment with Dr Barbour.’

Thomas had thought about seeing the calm woman with the steady hands and low voice, but he’d quickly realised there was no point. He was a rational, intelligent man, and after days and nights of concentrated thinking, every path of thought led to one conclusion: he was trapped. Talking couldn’t change that, no matter who you talked to. His first instinct had been that they needed to move house. Immediately. The house was where it had happened, where the men had found them, they should run for the hills. But he soon realised that the men weren’t interested in the house, they were only interested in him and wherever they went he was the target. They’d found him all the way out here; they could find him anywhere. As long as he worked with large amounts of money he would be at risk, his family would be at risk. As for the job, he needed the salary and wasn't qualified to do anything else; he'd never had a proper job in his life outside the bank.

Trapped.

He looked directly at his wife to tell her all this and saw that her cheeks were red and there was a thin line of sweat below her hairline. He looked at the still record on the turntable and realised. She'd been dancing! Fucking dancing! Thomas strode out of the room, slamming the door with such force the plaster around the frame cracked and spread like a struck eggshell.

Nine

Thomas's new temper was a shock to Ann. He'd arrived in her life all those years ago so cautiously, so gradually, and his calm presence had been a balm to her ever since. Conner Ryan had roared up to Ann on an orange and black motorbike, shook her to her core, shattered her and then sped off back to the other side of town. With Thomas there had been no revving engine, no outrageous beautiful looks, but he was handsome, gentle and good, and his timing was perfect.

In the weeks and months since her split from Conner Ann had been distant from her old set of friends. She couldn't stand their excitement, their eagerness to talk about how she'd been tragically wronged, and she spent more time working in the library at lunch, leaving for home as soon as her last class finished. And the less time she spent with them, the more she realised she didn't like them much anyway. Juliette, in particular, was spiteful and hard, and because the rest of the girls deferred to her it was easier to walk away from the lot of them. She received some grief. They had expected her to become part of their group again, they had been prepared to welcome her back after her desertion, but when Ann made it clear she wasn't interested in being welcomed back the bitching started. Ann didn't care; she was still concentrating on standing up without falling over, walking in the right direction. Most days she felt like a sandcastle facing the ocean. She didn't have the energy to contend with the spite of old friends.

It was a lonely summer. Ann spent her days working in a clothes shop, folding pastel-coloured jumpers, selling hideously patterned blouses to the over-fifties of Maltham.

'I suppose you wouldn't go for anything like this, would you love?' a woman might say, as she bagged contrastingly garish and meek selections. 'You would want something much more trendy, a young girl like you.' She would smile and shake her head, listen to them tell her about the wedding they were going to, the anniversary meal that was coming up, the cruise they'd anticipated for years. It was dull work but she enjoyed it. She was surprised how quickly the ladies took her into their confidence, how easily they shared, how funny they could be. Some customers spoke more to her over the course of buying new tights than her own mother did in a week. But she was keen to get back to her A levels, to lose her brain in work again. It was the first week of the autumn term when she first met Rebecca Norton, a new girl in her Classics set who'd only appeared that September. One night they confirmed their friendship with a visit to the cinema in Pulton. The film ran longer than expected and they came out into the dark night to find they'd missed the last bus home.

'I'll ring my dad,' Ann said, but Rebecca told her she would phone her brother. 'He's just passed his test, he's desperate for an excuse to drive,' she said.

Thomas arrived half an hour later, carefully negotiating the narrow streets of the town centre, indicating to an empty road that he was pulling in as soon as he spotted his sister up ahead. Rebecca and Ann chatted in the car but there was no conversation with Thomas. He was hunched forward in his seat, his hands firmly gripping the wheel in the ten-to-two position, his eyes flicking from the road in front to the mirror above him and quickly back to the road. When they reached Maltham Ann said goodbye to Rebecca and thanked the back of Thomas's head. 'Any time,' he said, his shoulders visibly relaxed now he'd stopped driving for a moment. Ann waved as she walked off and the car pulled slowly away – she hadn't even seen his face.

Ann and Rebecca went to see a film most weeks and when they stepped out of the foyer into the street Thomas would be waiting for them, flashing the lights of his dad's car.

'I told you,' Rebecca said, 'any excuse for a drive.'

Whenever Ann visited Rebecca it wouldn't be long before Thomas appeared, brushing his hair flat with a hand, hanging around the doorway of whatever room they happened to be in. 'Go away Thomas, leave us in peace,' Rebecca would say, raising her eyebrows to Ann and shaking her head.

But it was Rebecca who moved things along eventually. 'I think my brother has something he'd like to ask you, but he'd rather know the answer before he asks the question,' she said, one day after a class. 'He's quite careful like that.'

Carefulness appealed to Ann. In fact, Thomas appealed to Ann. The feelings had come as a surprise to her. She'd turned up at Rebecca's house one evening, where they were going to write their essays together. Ann greeted Rebecca's parents and then they settled down to work in the kitchen. After half an hour of being undisturbed Ann looked up from her work and said, 'Is Thomas not in tonight?'

'He's gone to work on a campsite in France for six weeks,' Rebecca told her.

'Thomas has?' Ann asked.

'I know! We couldn't believe it. He was homesick when he went camping with the Cubs for the weekend. And his French is non-existent.'

Ann laughed with Rebecca but it felt like clouds had settled in her chest and the clouds stayed for six weeks.

'Are you sure you don't mind?' Ann asked her friend the afternoon of the first date.

'Mind. Why would I mind?' Rebecca said. 'Although the thought of anyone going on a date with my brother baffles me.'

Ann didn't know why, but the things she liked about Thomas were the same things that drove Rebecca mad. 'He just appears! And then you turn to say something to him and he's already gone. He should have a bell on him. Like a cat.'

Ann admired this quiet and stealth. Most sixth-form boys wrestled with each other in the common room, chased each other out of the buildings and into the pubs, were always shouting across the street, bundling into cars and speeding off somewhere, arriving with a squeal of brakes and slamming doors. And Conner had been unable to make a quiet entrance or exit. His motorbike could be heard from streets away and then, when he arrived, he would be the centre of the room as soon as he entered it, the room would feel empty when he left. Sometimes, with Conner, it felt like you were in the only place in the world you should be. Sometimes it was too much. But Thomas, Thomas stood at the side of the room, he stayed close to the door, and you would wonder if he even knew himself that he was in the room. Ann welcomed the calm, the moderation of Thomas. And she quickly found out that he wasn't shy. At the end of their first date Thomas took hold of Ann's hand, pulled her to a stop and kissed her in the middle of the street. His determination, his directness, had taken Ann by surprise and her pulse was still racing when he dropped her off at home ten minutes later. That night as she settled herself in bed, she had to concede – it wasn't quite as thrilling as being kissed by Conner in the starlight, underneath her parents' bedroom window, but it wasn't far off. And she was older now; she was experienced, she understood the risks and dangers involved. Quieter love was still love.

Neither Thomas nor Rebecca knew anything about Conner. They'd arrived in town weeks after it had ended and Ann saw no point in telling them about it. But Maltham was a small town, Conner was always out, and a meeting was inevitable. It happened in the Swan and Royal. Ann and Thomas were both slightly drunk, holding hands across the table when a figure appeared above them. Thomas tried to pull his hand away, but seeing who was stood over them, Ann held on firmly.

'Hello,' Conner said.

'Hello,' Ann replied, hoping her face didn't flush, hoping Thomas couldn't feel her pulse rocketing through her thumb. 'This is Thomas.'

'Your boyfriend?'

'He is.'

Conner looked Thomas over. 'He seems nice,' he said, slyly, and walked out of the pub.

'Who was that?' Thomas asked.

'A guy I used to work with,' Ann said. 'An idiot.'

Thomas looked at the door Conner had disappeared through and said, 'Just work?'

'We went out, for a bit,' Ann said.

'Bloody hell.' Thomas shook his head.

Ann knew what he meant; Conner looked as good as ever.

'Were you serious?' Thomas asked.

'No, no. Just a few dates.'

It didn't feel like a lie or deceit to Ann. Dismissing the relationship was the only way she could feel any control over it. And she still barely had any control anyway. For the rest of the night she felt like it was the second after the start of a race, that she should be jostling and tearing forward, but here she was with Thomas and there was nowhere to run to.

She'd kept the details of her relationship with Conner, and the fallout, from Thomas deliberately, but she hadn't set out to convince him that she was a virgin, and by the time she understood Thomas believed that to be the case, it was too late.

'Are you alright?' he'd asked. 'Does it hurt?' he'd whispered as they moved together for the first time. And it was Thomas's first time and he was so happy – particularly after their second attempt when he showed more control and Ann had dug her nails into his back and pulled him into her as deep as he would go, holding him there and not allowing him to move, even when he was desperate to move.

Afterwards they'd rolled away from each other and Thomas had laughed like a school boy. 'Bloody hell,' he said wrapping his arms around her, 'bloody hell!' and laughed until Ann was infected by his laughter too. But then he'd fallen quiet and in the afternoon light of her drawn-curtained bedroom told her he loved her. Ann looked into his kind, hopeful face and was sure and said, 'I love you too.'

How could she tell him after that? Should she tell him that she and Conner had done it in the cellar of the pub? On the golf course? Against the back wall of the house whilst her parents slept upstairs? Should she tell him that she hadn't thought it was possible to feel the way she did, and then it was over and it was like having a block of flats collapse on top of her, but when the dust had cleared she was somehow still alive? It was better that he knew nothing about the whole mess of it.

Ann still felt guilt. Even now, years into their marriage, after two children, she would feel a surge of panic when she remembered Thomas thought she'd been a virgin when they met.

One night in bed, shortly after the move to Abbeystead, when they were sleeping together again, Thomas said to her, 'Do you ever wish you'd been with other men? Don't you worry that you've missed out? That other men might have been more adventurous? More exciting?'

Ann propped herself up on her elbow, looked at Thomas and said, 'I sometimes wonder if other men would have been bigger.'

Thomas's face was wiped clean of any expression, and then he saw Ann's smile and began to laugh.

'But what about you?' Ann asked, keen to move the conversation on. 'Don't you wish you'd had more sex with different women? Maybe I'm terrible. Maybe you could have been having much more fun with a different woman all these years.'

Thomas looked at the ceiling. 'I can't deny that, once or twice, over the years, I've noticed another woman.' He rolled on his side and put his arm around Ann and pulled her to him, resting his forehead against hers and quietening his voice. 'But I wouldn't swap a single second with you for a night with any of them.'

He held Ann's gaze and it took her a second to realise that he was taking his turn at joking, and she punched his arm as he laughed.

'It's true,' he said, in mock defence, 'not a single second,' and then they kissed each other good night and settled down to sleep. Ann turned on her side, relieved that the discussion was done, hopeful that the subject wouldn't crop up again for years.

It had been a happy marriage. Thomas treated her well, he was a kind, caring man, and, unlike her dad, he helped around the house and with the children. And sex with Thomas had been good enough. Not all-consuming, not always intense, but she had no complaints. Ann had occasionally thought of the sex with Conner, the urgent lustfulness of it, but over time it became something she couldn't properly remember any more, like a childhood holiday, or the face of her best friend who moved from her street when she was seven. Ann remembered the memory, but the details, the heat of it, were lost to her. And she wasn't a seventeen-year-old girl any more; sex against a wall or in the back of a car wasn't necessary. She had her own room, her own house; sex was no longer illicit. And maybe that was the difference. Sex as an infatuated teenager, in stolen moments, with an older boy from the other side of town, would never be the same as sex with her husband in their bedroom.

Not that there had been any sex recently. In the days after the robbery Thomas only touched her when he inspected her eye. He would pull her to the light, hold her head in his hands and peer at the bruised mess.

'I'm alright,' she told him, more than once. 'It bloody hurt, but I'm alright. Hundreds of people get punched, or worse, much worse, Thomas.'

'I know,' he would reply. 'It doesn't bear thinking about.'

But she suspected that he did think about it, that he thought about little else. There had been small changes in him over the years, particularly after they moved to Abbeystead. He'd always been a careful man, a neat man, but since the move to the forest he'd become . . . fussier, was the word. She could tell that he didn't like it when the children's toys were trailing throughout the house or when Harriet was painting at the kitchen table with paint-splattered newspaper spread out and sticky hands threatening. He would ask her if she'd finished as soon as she paused, dying to clear everything away, wash everything up. And he'd become intolerant of noise. The television or radio always had to be at a volume he didn't find intrusive. When they first got together they'd gone all over; they would travel across the country to see a band they both loved, but after the move it was hard enough to get Thomas to visit town. 'I'm there every day,' he would say. Which wasn't quite true, Ann thought. He was in the bank every day, which wasn't the same. The longer they spent in Bleasdale, the more its boundaries seemed to become Thomas's boundaries. 'Fancy a drink in Keasden?' he would say, clapping his hands together, as if a drink in the village pub was just the tonic they needed. None of that had concerned Ann too much, she accepted that people changed, and his goodness hadn't deserted him, but after the robbery the changes were manifest. He was curt with the children and dismissive with her. Since the night the men came he closed down, cut her off, went inside himself and brooded. If only he could see that it was a horrible, terrible night, but that it was over, Ann thought. But somehow he'd got it into his head that it was the start of a war, that men were planning another invasion, driving out to the trees, pulling on masks. Sometimes she wanted to shake him.

Ten

Keith set off later than he'd intended, the hangover was a bad one, and it was after four when he climbed into the car, still feeling unwell and jumpy. As he passed the cement works, heading for the bypass, he realised that he was leaving Etherton for the first time in a long time, the first time since the night of the robbery. He wondered if he should have been more adventurous with his cash. Many people who came into money, the first thought they had was of a foreign holiday, he knew. But for Keith the freedom from work was the holiday, the nights out provided him with the excitement. Still, it was something to consider. He did like the idea of Spain, warm sun and bars by the beach, or maybe even New York with its hustle and excitement, but as much as those places appealed, he couldn't envisage himself going. A few years ago in Spain he could have taken his shirt off, tanned himself on the beach, but not now, not with his stomach. He knew some men walked proudly, parading their belly without shame, slapping their stomachs contentedly and saying, 'It's all paid for,' but Keith was too vain. And although the thought of New York was exciting, he couldn't see himself there either. All those tall buildings cut through by wide streets. He would be lost in New York, he was too small, people wouldn't even notice him. And the women in films in New York always seemed as tall as the buildings they passed; skinny, lengthy women, walking quickly, hard faces and sharp clothes. New York women wouldn't have considered him even in his younger, thinner days. London made more sense, it was closer and cheaper, but London didn't mean anything to him. It was the capital of his country but he never thought about the place, he didn't see it as proper England. He'd been a couple of times for weekend binges with friends and hadn't liked it at all. He found the people cocky in their urgency, so he walked as quickly as everyone else, even when he was lost, keen to give the illusion that he knew what was what, that he had somewhere to be too. Lots of blacks too, proper blacks. There were pakis in northern towns, had been for years, but you tended not to see them that much, they had their own streets and schools and shops. They moved in and the whites moved out and everyone knew where they lived and you never had to go there. But in London you would be sat next to one on the tube, one would serve you in a shop. Keith didn't like that. He preferred to know who he was likely to meet before he met them. And if there was money in his pocket, he was happy drinking wherever happened to be nearest. Anyway, he thought, as he drove along the bypass – this was a trip of sorts.

Etherton fell away quickly. It hadn't spread much to the north where the cement works, the quarries and the industrial estate sat at the top of the town and soon he was passing fields. He'd thought about asking John along, but hadn't seen him properly for a while, and if he did bump into him in a pub or around town, John would quickly make his excuses and leave. Keith wondered if he was being careful after the robbery, but he suspected it was because of the woman. He knew some men could be funny about that; saw it as a mortal sin, hitting a woman. Keith couldn't see why. If you were prepared to punch a man, why wouldn't you punch a woman? Did men's noses not break? Did their skin not bruise? And some of the women who'd gone for him over the years, he would rather have been in a fight with a man. At least with a man there was no scratching. But Keith would apologise if necessary. He would admit it was the wrong thing to do if it would get John back onside. It would be good to have him for the job, a good man, a man who'd done it before.

It wasn't that he was planning to do it yet, but the money would run out and he would need more, so today he was making sure he could find the house again, find a place to leave the car. It would put his mind at rest to know where it all was. And if John was right, that months of work had gone into finding this man and his house, it seemed a shame to waste all that work on one job. Once he'd found the place he would drive home slowly, stop at a couple of country pubs and be back in Etherton in time for an evening session. He was already looking forward to that. The beer would taste like he'd earnt it.

Fifteen minutes into the drive Keith was dropping down a gear and heading up Marshaw Fell. He glanced around him as he drove, at the fields on either side, the stone walls scaling impossible slopes, the desperate-looking trees shaken by hill winds. The area was popular with walkers, bird watchers, cyclists, fell runners, nature lovers. None of it made any sense to Keith; the countryside unsettled him. He was a man used to street lights, shops and signs. In winter the dark fells surrounding Etherton spooked him. He imagined being stuck on one of them at dusk in December, dark and cold coming in, mist settling, hiding the lights of any villages and farmhouses. If he had to choose countryside or London, dirty, arrogant London would win every time.

Finding the forest wasn't difficult, but as soon as he entered the trees he was lost. He'd only been to the house when he was driven there, the night they held the family, and when they left in the morning he wasn't driving then either, John was, and he'd paid no attention to the route taken – he was tired, and full of adrenaline from punching the woman, excited about the money he couldn't quite believe was going to be his. He could hardly remember the journey at all. So he drove slowly through the forest, searching for the house, crawling along tiny roads with sudden steep climbs and unexpected drops. There were more houses than he expected, but most were easy to dismiss. He remembered the house he was looking for was newer than the ones he was passing; it was more modern than the farmhouses with small windows and grey stones, bigger too. The stonework wasn't weathered and he remembered large windows going all the way to the floor. Rich people windows. He drove down every road he could find, no matter how small or unpromising, and several times he found himself turning his car around in the front yard of a house after finding himself at another dead end. He'd been driving under the trees for an hour and was about to give up when he hit the cat. It was a grey cat, young and thin, and it was out of the hedgerow and under his wheels before he could react. It was a slight thump; there was hardly any movement in his arms or his hands on the steering wheel. He stopped the car, climbed out and crouched down and saw the animal underneath – as dead as if it had never been alive. He saw a silver glint at the cat's throat. 'Shit,' he said. There was a red collar and hanging off the collar was a tag.

He recoiled a couple of times, he didn't want to touch the dead thing, but he made himself pull the cat from under the car by its belly. The left eye had popped out and was hanging by a strand of pale flesh, there was blood around the ear and the mouth and the teeth were bared as if it was about to attack. He looked at the silver tag and read, 'Lewis. Bank Hill Cottage.' He stood up, turned around and saw, back along the road, behind the hedge, a cottage.

Keith pushed the cat to the side of the road with his feet and walked to the driver's door. He rested his hands on the roof of the car. 'Shit,' he said, again, and pulled off his jumper.

He opened the boot, knelt at the side of the road, wrapped the jumper around the cat and lifted him up. He was about to place him in the boot but it was a mess, empty cans, sweet wrappers and old newspapers spread out in there. He lowered the cat back to the road, gathered the rubbish in his arms and dropped it onto the back seat. Then he laid the cat in the boot. He turned the car in the narrow lane, drove back the way he'd come and paused at the driveway to the cottage. A small, oval wooden sign was attached to a gatepost. 'Bank Hill,' it said. Keith drove up the steep drive to the cottage.

He turned off the engine and sat there.

What was he going to say? People loved their animals.

Then he noticed a woman at the front door, stood with her arms folded. She was looking over at Keith. He opened his door. 'I'm sorry,' he said, climbing out.

The woman walked forward. 'Can I help?' she asked.

Keith held his arms out at his side and said, 'Your cat. I'm sorry. I killed your cat.'

The woman looked at Keith and then to the road and Keith said, 'He's in the boot.'

He opened the boot and the woman walked forward with her right hand on her chest and when she saw her cat, its body wrapped in a blue jumper, blood dripping from its open mouth, she said, 'Oh.' She rested her hands against the rim of the boot and her head dropped.

'He was underneath me before I saw him,' Keith said. 'I couldn't have missed him.'

The woman lifted the cat from the car and carried him into the house.

Keith stayed where he was, he wondered if he should leave, but that seemed the wrong thing to do. A young woman on a horse passed slowly along the road below him, smiling at him as she went, the steady noise of the hooves on the road the only sound in the air. A few minutes later the woman came out of the house, she was holding his jumper out to him, she'd been crying. 'I rinsed it,' she said. 'But it will need a good wash.'

Keith shook his head. 'Throw it away, I don't want it.'

The woman nodded and lowered the jumper.

'My husband is driving the children back in a few minutes,' she said. 'They would have found him there, so thank you, for bringing him to us.'

Keith shook his head and said, 'I'm sorry.' Tears were in his eyes now.

'You were kind to bring him home.' The woman

turned and went back into the house.

Keith drove back to Etherton slowly. His eyes scanned the edges of the roads for any stray animals. He thought about the cat, about how unlucky it had been. Perhaps the only time in his life he would drive down that road and the cat chose that moment to run out. Life was fragile, Keith thought. Then he decided he needed a drink.

Eleven

When Thomas came home from work he closed the front door behind him, stood still and listened. He hated to hear silence. He wanted noise from the kitchen, Harriet singing in her bedroom, even Ann shouting at Daniel, anything to suggest that all was well. When he was reassured that the men were not back he called his hellos to the children, found Ann and kissed her quickly on the cheek. Then he preferred silence. The children would be told to turn the television down, to play quietly. If the noise continued he would become short-tempered, storm about like an angry king, upset the children and infuriate Ann. Through his temper and persistence the family learnt it was easier to be quiet when Dad was home. Thomas was left bewildered by their behaviour. He couldn't understand why they weren't listening for the crunch of feet on gravel, the next knock at the door.

After eating Thomas would retreat to his office

upstairs. Here he studied the security tape recorded by the camera outside the front door. He poured himself a drink from the bottle in his filing cabinet, rewound the tape, pressed fast forward and watched intently as the screen flickered away in front of him. The camera picked up the road and the edge of the forest, so nobody could use the road or approach the house without Thomas having a record of it. But the house was so remote Thomas was mostly watching a fast-forwarded picture of an empty road. Occasionally a car passed and Thomas would pause the tape and make a note of the time, the make and model of the car, the registration number where possible, the direction the car was travelling and anything about the occupants that he could see, any clues to their age or sex. He kept a magnifying glass in his drawer, which he sometimes needed for dirty number plates and blurry occupants. He looked to see if the car slowed or showed any interest in the house as it passed. When all the information was recorded he would work through his previous entries to see if the vehicle had made an appearance before and, if it had, when and how many times. This information was transferred to a large sheet he kept folded up at the back of his notebook. Occasionally he'd be able to identify the car as belonging to someone in the village, and that pleased him, it was one less entry to worry about. But every journey would still be recorded, even Mrs Silverwood's trips to and from the village. Thomas put this down to his training in the bank – record everything accurately all the time. He found it satisfying to gather this information and put it away in columns, in order.

There was a separate section in his notebook for people passing on foot or bike. Cyclists were not uncommon at weekends, walkers less so; they tended to stick to the popular routes – picturesque paths along rivers, long climbs with rewarding views, but the odd hiker would pass, solid boots striding firmly along the road. Their age, height and sex would be recorded along with the date and time. Thomas was shocked early on in viewing the tapes when he saw a man, at one in the morning, making his way towards the house – a black thing evolving out of the darkness. He was flooded with anxiety until he noticed the man's stiff gait, understood the size of him as he came closer and realised that it was Raymond on one of his night walks. As Raymond passed the house his hand came out of his pocket and he gave a small wave to the camera. Thomas waved back instinctively. How wonderful it would be, he thought, to have Raymond patrolling every night, up and down the road, his eyes searching for moving shadows in the trees, someone else taking the burden so Thomas could sleep the sleep he used to, when his family was safe, his home unbreached. Every time Raymond appeared on one of the recordings in the middle of the night, Thomas felt a glimmer of hope.

Ann knew what he was doing. He'd tried to do it without her realising, telling her he was catching up on work, acting on the latest diktat from head office, but she'd walked in on him and caught him red-handed. Thomas scrambled to stop the video but he was too slow. His face flushed and he sat there feeling as guilty as if he was caught watching pornography. Ann looked down at him, his notebook with its headings and columns open on his lap and said, 'We need to talk, Thomas,' and left the room. But they didn't talk and Thomas carried on, notebook open, whisky at his side, staring at the screen, looking for the men.

Thomas did manage to keep his forest surveillance a secret from Ann. The men had parked up in the forest and come through the trees, it was the only thing the police were sure of. They'd told Thomas that the house would likely have been watched for a period before the men struck, so instead of walking every morning like he used to, Thomas searched the forest for clues. He looked for footprints in the mud, for freshly discarded litter (although he doubted the leader would allow any litter dropping). He dropped to his hands and knees to inspect the threads he'd tied between certain trees, to see if any had been disturbed or broken. There were never any footprints other than his own, never any litter, and the threads remained undisturbed until one heart-stopping morning, weeks into his checks. It was a morning when the mist had settled around the base of the trees and the forest looked miraculous and unearthly. The trunks of the trees were so obscured that Thomas thought he must be mistaken when he found the broken thread, but a closer inspection clearly showed the snapped end trailing on the forest floor. He tried not to panic; it could have been anything – a fox, a deer, a fallen branch. But then he saw a footprint cut into the forest floor and panic threw itself at him.

The realisation didn't catch him until the afternoon, when he was in his office, attempting to concentrate on writing staff appraisals. It was an obvious thought but in his panic it had taken him hours to arrive there: Raymond. It had been months since they'd last seen each other and in that time Thomas's brain had been rushed with anxiety, his muscles as hard as bone, it was all he could do to shower and get to work. Other than the occasional sighting on the security camera he hadn't thought of Raymond at all. But after he finished work that day he drove straight to the Chapman farm and Raymond's caravan. He approached the caravan slowly, his eyes cast to the ground, searching for footprints, but the ground was too hard to show him any evidence. He looked further ahead and saw the grass had worn away at the foot of the caravan door. It wasn't quite mud, but there was enough yield in the land to leave a footprint from a large boot. There were five or six of them, large and clear, the exact same footprint Thomas had seen in the forest that morning, he was sure of it. Thomas felt exhausted in his relief. He straightened his back, let out a deep breath and decided to leave without knocking on Raymond's door. But before he had time to turn and walk away the caravan door was pulled open and Raymond shoved his head out of the dark hatch. When he saw Thomas in front of him a wide smile opened his face. 'Thomas!' he said, looking as pleased as if Thomas was stood there holding a large present up to him. Thomas was itching to get home, this detour had already delayed him by twenty minutes and he wanted to be back, to check that everyone was well, to check that nobody was a hostage. He looked up at Raymond's happy, expectant face and said, 'Come to the house?'

That night, in the garden, loosened by wine and beer, Thomas told Raymond what had happened the night the men had come. He'd told the police of course, but they'd needed times and descriptions, they were after clues and the truth of it had been lost in the detail. And when he arrived home from the bank he'd told Ann about everything that had happened, and asked what had happened at the house, although the battered eye already told him. But he'd never talked freely, truthfully, about the fear, the dread he'd felt when he'd realised what was happening.

'I didn't understand how safe I'd felt until this happened,' he said. 'There have been problems along the way, it's not like I've been ecstatic all my life, but I've never felt like this before. Now I can't leave the house or come home without feeling terrified.'

He described the men coming into the house, taking control like a cat lifting a kitten by its scruff. 'They walked in,' he said, 'without a word. And then we were just sitting there, with them in a line in front of us, all night. And then in the morning I had to go with them to the bank. I didn't want to leave Ann and the children, but by going I was helping to bring it to an end, and there was no choice anyway. If I'd made any fuss think about what they might have done. The only thing for me to do was to help them get the money.'

'Did they hurt you?' Raymond asked.

'One of them smashed Ann in the face before they left. Really punched her.'

Thomas looked at Raymond. 'Just . . .' His face hung loose. 'But the men with me treated me fine. They drove me to the bank, parked at the front and walked me in. I did everything they told me to because they had guns. It was easy. And whilst there was always the threat they might shoot me after they got what they wanted, I didn't ever really feel that they would. After I gave them the money they locked me in the cleaning cupboard.'

Thomas watched a small fly hover around the sticky brim of his glass.

'But when they had gone, it only really started then. When it's happening you are just trying to get to the end of it. After it's happened, it becomes something else. When I saw what they'd done to Ann . . .'

'That must have been terrible,' said Raymond.

Thomas nodded. 'But everyone seems to be coping. The children, they were distraught when it all happened and upset for a while afterwards, but they are getting on with things now. It's like they had a bug and they've shaken it off. Ann, she just won't let it affect her. It's like she's made of steel. I'm the wreck.'

Thomas looked over to Raymond again.

'Do you know what I'm doing? I'm keeping a record of every car, every person that passes the house. I'm going into the woods and searching for any clues that they've been back.' He shook his head. 'Ann thinks I'm mad,' he said, looking into the trees. 'She thinks I'm losing it.'

'Well, you're being careful,' Raymond said. 'It's understandable after everything that's happened. Have you seen anything suspicious?'

Thomas smiled at Raymond and said, 'Apart from your footprint? In truth, not really, no. But then, who knows? And if it does happen again, I've got the tapes and records to refer to. To show the police.'

'I don't think they'll come back,' said Raymond.

'People say that,' said Thomas. 'It's an easy thing to say. It doesn't really mean anything. But to live here . . . I almost wish I knew they were coming back. So

I could prepare. The waiting and watching, it's exhausting.' He drained his glass of wine. 'Ann thinks I should see someone. A psychiatrist.'

Thomas looked at Raymond. 'Do you think it's mad? What I'm doing, after what happened? To be worried? To think they might come back?'

'No,' Raymond said firmly. 'Not at all. I think you're doing the right thing. You're trying to protect your family.'

Thomas thanked him and they drank on in silence, the darkness coming in quickly, shutting down Abbeystead for the night.

It became their new arrangement – drinks at the house, or drinks in the back garden if the weather allowed. Thomas didn't want to leave Ann and the children to go on long walks or sit in the pub, and Raymond seemed happy enough to come to the house. Initially Raymond only visited on Thursday nights, but Thomas liked having him around, another man in the house calmed him a little, made him feel like he had back-up, he was happy to admit, so he invited him more often and Raymond would visit several times a week. At first Raymond was shy around the family. Thomas smiled at how polite he was, even with the children. Harriet would rush over to him and say, 'Raymond! Are you alright?' And six foot six Raymond would blush a little, bow his head and say, 'I'm well Harriet, how are you?' as reverent as if he was talking to the Queen. Ann encouraged Raymond to come over in time for their evening meal and he would often stay until the family was in bed, until it was just him and Thomas in the back garden finishing their drinks. When they were done Raymond would walk to the bottom of the garden and into the trees and back to his caravan. Thomas would head up to his office to catch up on his security videos and finish the night off with some whisky before going to bed in the early hours. The sleep, even with the whisky in him, was never deep or restful, but at least it wasn't consciousness. He wasn't listening to the trees stretch and crack and hearing men shouldering his front door.

Part Three

One

They had been the bane of his life. He dreamt of them gone, and then they were. Keith came back from the pub one night to find the house silent, the wardrobes empty. A letter arrived a week later. Rose was living with another man, they were in love, and he'd agreed to take the girls in also. No return address was included in the letter, no phone number either. Keith decided to drink, but the money from the job was now so slender it almost fit into his wallet, so he bought cheap bottles from the off licence and drank in the house. Keith ventured into town a couple of times in the week after the letter arrived, but had to rush back home when he realised tears were coming and couldn't be stopped. Slowly, over several tearful drunk days, it dawned on Keith that he was heart-broken. It was a twist in the tale he couldn't have predicted, he was stunned when he realised – he loved Rose. Once he'd understood and digested this shocking fact, Keith crumbled. He wept for Rose, he dreamt of her. He spent hours imagining her and her new lover, a tall, muscular man, consummating their relationship noisily and at length, in all the ways he and Rose had never done, in every room of the man's expensive house. He heard ecstatic, guttural noises emerging from Rose, noises that Keith had never provoked in all their years of disappointing, clumsy, half-drunk love-making, when the only aim had been his own feeble climax and blessed sleep for both of them. After torturing himself in this way for days Keith hit the pubs of Etherton, intent on finding a man who looked how he imagined Rose's new lover to look. In his third pub, when he was suitably drunk, he found him. A man ten years his junior, tall and tanned, his T-shirt clinging to his wide chest, falling away again at the flat stomach. The man was surrounded by a group of friends, all in T-shirts and jeans too. Keith turned back to his drink and wondered when it had become the fashion to head out for a night dressed so casually. He felt disdain for such sloppiness and was sadly aware that he, in his suit and tie, would be considered the one dressed foolishly by these men. Rose's lover finished telling a story to the gathered men and the group erupted into laughter. Keith slammed his drink down on the bar. They were fucking laughing at him.

He approached the man with his fists raised to the ceiling in the manner of an old-time boxer. His intended opponent looked at the portly little drunk in front of him and laughed.

'What do you want?' he asked.

'Come on,' Keith said. 'Let's go, come on.'

The man looked around at his friends and laughed again. 'I'm not going to fight you,' he said, holding his arms out from his side in a gesture of reason and peace.

At that moment Keith lunged forward clumsily and attempted to punch the man in the stomach. The man stepped aside gracefully and Keith stumbled into a table and fell to the floor. The man bent down, picked him up, put him over his shoulder and carried him out of the pub like a sack of potatoes, Keith's fists raining down ineffectively on his back, the man's friends cheering and laughing as they went.

Keith was carried into the alley at the side of the pub and put down, quite gently.

'We're not really going to fight, are we?' the man asked.

Keith, all fight gone from him, slumped into the wall and slid to his haunches.

'Go home and sleep it off,' the man said, and turned and walked away.

'You don't even love her!' Keith cried out to the disappearing back. 'You can't love her like I do!'

Keith wept in the alley before he pulled himself up and staggered off to find another drink. Settled in the corner of a quiet pub with a fresh pint he considered it all. He had no idea where Rose had gone, and that was the cruellest thing. He'd been cut off. If only he knew where she was he could have gone to her, made his case, begged her to come back. He could have tidied himself up, lost some weight, even got a job. He would wear jeans and a T-shirt if that was what she wanted.

In a sober moment two days later, when the headache had cleared enough for Keith to think without feeling sick, he considered his options. He wanted Rose back and she wouldn't consider returning if he didn't have a job, and whilst in the middle of his drinking and money days, when the cash left his wallet ripe and heavy in his pocket, the thought of having to return to work made him recoil, now that Rose was gone and he knew heartbreak, the thought of working for a living didn't haunt him like it had in his glory days. He was alone and hopeless, of course he should be crawling to work every day like everyone else; he deserved no less. He was a broken man.

But it was only when a sober Keith looked in the mirror he realised how broken he was. His skin was Etherton sky grey, and apart from the thin red tributaries that crisscrossed his cheeks, flooding his nose, there was no colour to him at all. His neck was beginning to absorb his chin, the fat was winning and he was being swallowed by it. He was mortified that the hair he'd been so proud of throughout his life, the hair that had seemed so thick, as steadfast as a mountain, was leaving him, seemingly as quickly as Rose had. He woke one morning to find his pillow covered in a thin blanket of hair. For a few seconds he wondered where it could have come from before the obvious, chilling realisation struck him. Still not believing it to be possible he ran a hand over his scalp and pulled it away to find a clutch of lifeless threads dancing between his fingers, as fine and destructible as a spider's web. The plughole was clogged with it too. His hair wasn't backing off slowly and kindly, leaving him with a dignified widow's peak; this was mass evacuation, and suddenly his scalp was showing itself at him from all angles. Keith felt a shot of fear. Was this who he was now? This fat, balding man looking back at him? He took to running the hot tap to steam the mirror so he didn't have to look at himself when he cleaned his teeth and washed his face. He had enough to contend with.

Two

Since Chapman's first hospital visit Raymond had been required at the farm more and more, and there were no long periods in Etherton, sitting and sleeping in his hated house, spending days dreaming of the dark forest and fells, hiding from his chaotic neighbours. Raymond was never told what illness had brought Chapman down, and his occasional questions were fielded vaguely by Sheila, and whilst Chapman did recover, he never fully regained the strength needed to work a farm. Chapman would rise at the same time as Raymond and they would talk over the work for the day and then Chapman would take on the light duties and after lunch he would remain inside, where Raymond suspected he slept most of the afternoon. It was Sheila who renegotiated Raymond's wages, under strict guidance from Chapman, Raymond understood, and whilst his hours may have almost doubled, his salary certainly didn't. Raymond accepted the money offered.

He realised he could have earned more working fewer hours in a supermarket, stocking shelves, but he wasn't in a supermarket with hundreds of customers and colleagues everywhere, joking or not joking, meaning what they said or the opposite. He was outside in Abbeystead, miles away from Etherton. Despite the pitiful salary and Chapman's permanent black mood, having regular work in Abbeystead made Raymond as happy as he expected he would ever be.

The house troubled him. It was always there, crawling underneath all his other thoughts, ambushing him when he finally began to fall into sleep. Every few weeks he went back to check the place, to collect what few pieces of post had arrived and clear the junk mail into the bin. He hated having to go, but he hated imagining what might have become of the place in his absence even more. It was always a relief when he turned the corner on to Granville Road to see the house was still standing at least. When he entered the front room he would see the carpets glittered with slug trails, smell the damp and cold air and try not to despair. Most of all he dreaded bumping into his next-door neighbours. A good visit was getting in and out without seeing Keith Sullivan or his girls, arriving back at the caravan without his pulse racing.

There hadn't been a visitor to the house in years, but Raymond preferred it that way, he was ashamed of the place and the state he'd allowed it to fall into. But when Thomas had asked him what he was planning for the weekend and Raymond told him he would be visiting the house, Thomas offered to drive him.

'Ann says I need to get out of the house. She's convinced I'm going mad.'

Raymond tried to brush the offer away.

'How long does it take on your bike?' Thomas asked.

'An hour or so,' Raymond said. 'The hills slow you down.'

'We'll be there in twenty minutes in the car, twenty-five at most. There and back in an hour or so. We can stop off for a pint on the way back.'

Raymond was powerless to refuse, but he dreaded to think what Thomas would make of his home. A man who lived like Thomas standing in his house was unimaginable.

Abbeystead was deep in mist the morning they set off but at the top of Marshaw Fell they broke through into a bright day and the sun stayed with them all the way to Etherton. The strong light and blue sky brought clarity to the ugliness of the place and as they passed through the outskirts of the town Raymond became so embarrassed he squirmed in his seat. With Thomas beside him all the faults and ugliness he usually put to the back of his mind leapt out at him. How had he come to own a house in a town like this? They passed boarded-up shops and pubs, rows of small, red-brick houses, many with sale and to let signs, sticking out like frozen flags. They passed a row of shops along the bottom of a grey precinct, two charity shops, a bookie's, an off licence and then more boarded-up windows. Graffiti covered the boards, slogans and symbols that meant nothing to Raymond.

And the people.

Raymond didn't judge, he was in no position, but he saw. Everyone in Etherton was either bone-thin or bulging out. It was a hopeless place.

'Not the nicest part of the world,' Raymond said.

'Oh, I don't know,' Thomas replied. 'I've seen worse.'

Raymond didn't believe him.

Raymond directed Thomas from the main road and

down a grid of thin streets to Granville Road. He noticed that the street he lived on didn't look too bad compared to the town they'd just driven through. The houses were neat and well maintained, a couple even had hanging baskets at the front and flowers in the window. 'I'm eleven, on the left,' Raymond said and pointed. 'The scruffy one.' Thomas drove along the street and pulled up outside Raymond's house. Both men sat and stared for a few seconds before Raymond unbuckled his seat belt.

'Shall I wait here?' Thomas asked.

Raymond sighed. He had wondered about asking Thomas to stay in the car, but now they'd arrived it seemed less urgent to keep the state of his house a secret. 'You might as well see it,' he said. 'But it's worse on the inside,' he warned.

He turned his key in the lock and pushed the door open, sweeping back a scattering of post. He flicked on the light switch and the bulb flashed and popped and the room shot back into darkness. They walked through to the next room and here the light bulb held. The house was as cold as Abbeystead on a winter morning.

'This is the kitchen through here,' said Raymond as he slid open a door onto a small square space at the back of the room. He peered out of the window and was surprised to see a clean backyard, his dustbin upright.

Thomas smiled at him. 'It's a good space, isn't it. High ceilings.'

Raymond shook his head. It was kind of Thomas to find something nice to say but he couldn't think a single good thought about the house.

'It's a wreck. Years ago I wanted to sell it, I wanted rid, and they did a survey and found damp in the walls and underneath the floorboards. That would have to be sorted first and there is no central heating. It would cost thousands before you looked at redecorating.'

'It does smell a bit damp,' Thomas conceded. 'Central heating would probably help dry it out. Have you thought about applying for a grant? You can get help with that sort of thing sometimes.'

'So much needs doing, I don't know where to start. And there is no money to even start with it all. I try not to think of the place.'

'Could you cut your losses and sell it as it is? Let the buyer do all the work?'

Raymond looked around at the house he owned and couldn't imagine that there was a single person in the world who would give him money for it. And, more depressingly, he would need somewhere to live one day.

'It's all I've got,' he said. 'I doubt the Chapmans are going to keep the farm going forever.' He trailed off. He'd voiced his biggest fear – that the farm would be run down and retired and he would be out of work and required to leave the caravan. He didn't know about the finances of the farm, but he knew that over the years Chapman had earned less, and now with Raymond doing most of the work, even less. And Chapman was getting older and had been ill; it wasn't a situation that would continue forever. To try and shake off the chill that had settled in him Raymond said, 'I'll just check upstairs,' and disappeared up the dark staircase. He glanced in both bedrooms and the bathroom. As he shoved his head through the bathroom door he saw that the damp patch on the bathroom ceiling had bloomed. It was the size of a dartboard now, and the ceiling looked spongy and vulnerable where the stain grew. Raymond closed the door. It was another reason to put the house from his thoughts as much as he could. He returned down the stairs and made sure the back door was locked and gathered the post, shoving the few addressed envelopes into his coat pocket. Raymond and Thomas stepped onto the pavement, the day feeling warmer now they'd been in a cold house. As they drove down the street they passed a paunchy man walking slowly, unsteadily, up the road. If it hadn't been for his shortness and leather jacket Raymond wouldn't have recognised him as his neighbour. How he'd aged. Thomas didn't notice the man at all.

Three

Keith was relieved to arrive home. After days of drinking he felt unwell and needed to sleep. His back had begun to spasm, locking him in pain, and his left eye felt tender and hot. He couldn't remember if he'd been in a fight or if his injuries were from a fall and he didn't care either way; he was bone-tired and only wanted sleep. He crawled up the stairs and dropped onto his messy bed with a heavy groan. As he lay there in the cold sheets Keith was hit by a clear and simple thought: this isn't living. Feeling sick and tired all the time isn't how most people experience life. That afternoon and into the night Keith dreamed of the mundane. He dreamt he was sober and ate a good meal. He dreamt he had a job. His job was to sweep clean the forecourt of a garage. When people passed on the street they waved to him and he would raise his brush in response. In the morning, with the hangover holding him firmly in its rusty jaws, Keith remembered the dream and wanted to return there, to escape his poisoned body. He wanted Rose to walk in the room and tell him everything would be alright.

The next day Keith walked to the nearest shop. He walked slowly, he had to, the pavement rose and fell unexpectedly, his legs dropped and bandied like he was crossing a bouncy castle. The air manhandled him, rushing at his skin. When he finally reached the shop he pushed the door, but he struggled to open it, it felt as heavy as a ship. Once inside Keith attempted to focus, but he was dazed by the brightness of lights, the busyness of the shelves. He'd been staring at trays of fruit for five minutes when an assistant called the manager and the young man arrived and asked Keith if he needed any help. Eventually, with the help of the manager, Keith found his basket full of the items he'd come to the shop to buy – cans of soup, bread, vitamin tablets, apples and bananas, no drink. He was exhausted after the short trip and went straight back to bed.

Recovery was slow in coming. In the mornings his body punished him as if he'd been on a session the night before. Sweat flooded from all surfaces of his body. Surely ankles shouldn't sweat? Keith wondered, but his did, his feet too. A pain would strike his kidneys as if they had been punched and more than once he clutched his stomach as its contents surged, and he had to surge to the toilet. On one trip to the shop he was too far from home when the dreaded kick hit, and it was a shamefaced Keith who hurried stiltedly back to Granville Road. On the third day without drink he was shivering. It was a warm day but Keith's skin felt as if it was being pricked by hundreds of ice-cold needles. His arms and legs ached until he didn't know where to put them. On the fourth day he stayed in bed, haunted by feelings of anxiety and dread. He lay there, his heart hammering against the mattress. He wondered if he was dying more than once. Sleep was his only escape and even then nightmares sometimes came and rocked him. It took another few days until he started to recover, until his body and mind calmed, and finally Keith felt able to venture outside again. He was still weak but the air was kinder to him now, it eased over his face, the sun warmed his body. He walked to a park and sat on a bench and watched the dog walkers and the mums and toddlers. He stretched his legs and enjoyed feeling present in the day. Then he was standing on his feet. He saw a short, brown-haired woman on the other side of the park, in a yellow coat, walking quickly, hurriedly, in his direction. When he understood it wasn't Rose he sat down suddenly. He felt the pain of a mouse in a trap. The downside of sobriety: there was no cushion between himself and reality.

Over the next few days Keith went from business to business in Etherton, offering himself in whatever capacity they might need him. Receptionists, foremen and managers all took his name and number, saying they would pass on his details, they would be in touch if something came up. They were all friendly enough, polite enough, but his phone didn't ring. Keith didn't give up. He understood the world wouldn't make it easy for him to be a different man to the man he'd been for so many years. In his head, to help him through, he kept up a dialogue with Rose. She was supportive and encouraging, she was proud of him and the changes he was trying to make. It kept him going to think like that. After Keith had tried all the businesses in town he drove to the trading estate behind the cement works. He parked his car on the side of the wide, smooth road and approached the first building. He left his name and number at each of the units he visited, but there was nothing going at any of them. He was about to head home when he saw a van pull out of a warehouse further up the road – a larger building than any other on the estate. 'EveryFrame' it said on the side of the van, in smooth bright green letters. Keith had heard about them – they fitted double glazing and built conservatories, they were always in the *Etherton Advertiser*, winning awards or raising money for local charities. In the accompanying photograph there would be five or six men in EveryFrame T-shirts, smiling and holding up thumbs for the camera. Keith walked to the huge brown shed of a building and headed for a small door on the side of the unit. He opened the door onto a smart reception room where comfy chairs rested neatly around a low table with flowers and magazines arranged on top. He let the door close behind him and a young girl looked up from behind her desk.

'Can I help?' she asked. She only looked the same age as his eldest daughter, but here she was, smart and smiling, wanting to help.

'I'm seeing if there are any jobs going,' Keith said, trying to smile back as openly as the girl smiled at him.

'I know they're after a couple of fitters. They're going through CVs. If you drop yours off I'll pass it on to HR.'

The girl gave Keith another quick smile before

picking up her phone, but when she saw Keith hadn't moved away she stopped dialling.

'Was there anything else?'

'I haven't really got a CV,' Keith said. 'I was just hoping to have a chat with someone.'

'They won't see you without a CV. Can't you just type one up and print it off?'

'Well, the computer's not working at the minute,' Keith said.

'The library,' the girl said happily. 'They'll sort you out. It'll only cost 10p to print.'

She smiled her last smile, picked up the phone and dialled.

Keith left frustrated. On the drive home he imagined what Rose would say. She would tell him to get himself to the library.

The next morning he woke without a trace of a hangover. It was still an unusual feeling for him and he savoured it. He felt light on his feet, he had an appetite, but there was something else; he felt an energy inside him that hadn't been there for years. He wanted to move, to get out of the house, to be in the world. He wanted to do something. The strangest feeling of all was not wanting a drink. Not drinking was giving him the same buzz that drinking had years before, when it was still exciting, when it still opened up a world of promise. He strode into town but his optimism quickly floundered at Etherton library. Creating a CV, it turned out, was not a simple matter, particularly for a man who had never used a computer before, had no idea how they worked and wasn't even sure what a CV was exactly. He managed to book himself some time on a PC, but didn't have a clue what to do with it, and with people typing away on either side of him, one lady old enough to be his mother, he felt foolish and a fraud. He stood up to leave just as a librarian approached and asked if he needed help. Keith explained what he had come to do and confessed, quietly, that he didn't know where to start. The librarian told Keith to write down all the jobs he'd had and the responsibilities they entailed and then, under the guise of giving him a lesson in word processing, quickly typed up the notes, correcting the spelling as he went. 'It's no masterpiece,' the librarian said, as the printer chugged out the paper, 'but it might help.' Keith left the library with five crisp copies of a CV.

The next day he drove to the industrial estate and dropped off his CV with the smiling receptionist at EveryFrame. She remembered him and promised to deliver the CV to the correct person. Keith drove home thinking about how helpful everyone had been. He should have stopped drinking years ago, he thought, if this was how people treated a sober, striving man. His luck continued later that night. When he was sorting through his clothes he found over £100 in the pocket of a jacket he hadn't worn for months. Money that would previously have gone on drink was spent on another food shop. More fruit, a few slices of meat, even some vegetables. When he was leaving the shop with his full bags he passed rows of magazines and a cover brought him to a halt. It was a huge white ship sailing across a flat blue sea. A cruise. Rose had always wanted to go on a cruise but Keith had never been interested. He wanted towns and cities, pubs and clubs, but he could see it now – both of them lying on a ship crossing an ocean. Walking past white buildings in a foreign town under a fierce sun, back to the ship at night, sailing through the warm dark, looking up at stars, holding hands. When he had the money in his pocket he would book that cruise. Before he bought food or clothes he would go to the travel agent's and book a cruise, then he would find Rose, give her the tickets and she would kiss him. Keith could see it.

Four

It was a week after Raymond and Thomas had visited his house when Sheila found him in the shippen. She asked Raymond to come across to the kitchen for a talk when he was done. She held her arms crossed over her chest as she spoke, as if protecting herself against a chill, but it wasn't cold at all. Raymond went back to his work feeling weak. He'd never been called to the house before for a talk. He couldn't decide whether to finish the work quickly and get the meeting over with or take his time and delay whatever was coming. After ten minutes of worry he pulled the shippen door closed behind him and walked over to the house. They sat at the kitchen table with Frank nowhere to be seen, but Raymond knew he would be behind one of the closed doors close by, listening. Sheila's face was drawn, she didn't offer Raymond a drink. They chatted about the jobs Raymond had planned for the day and then, as if they were still talking about the broken cattle grid, she was saying she was sure it wasn't unexpected, that Raymond must have realised, particularly with Frank's health as it was . . . She stopped. She hit one hand with the other, and, like a diver jumping off a board, threw herself into it.

'We've had to sell the farm, Raymond. It's breaking Frank's heart.'

Raymond didn't say anything.

'Do you understand, Raymond?' Sheila asked. 'The farm won't be ours. There won't be a job.'

Raymond did understand. Seven days before, he'd spoken to Thomas about his worst fear and now it was being delivered to him.

'Raymond?' Sheila said, looking for a response.

'Where will you go?' Raymond asked. He couldn't imagine Chapman anywhere other than on this farm and in this house.

'We'll stay here. But we're selling the land and the cattle to the Whitwells.'

Raymond looked up. 'Maybe they'll need—' he said, but Sheila was already shaking her head.

'Whatever you think of Frank he did his best for you,' she said. 'He tried to get them to take you, but it's the Whitwells, Raymond.'

The Whitwells. Raymond understood. Three strong sons and all the equipment a farm could ever need, no matter how big. Chapman wouldn't have even mentioned Raymond's name.

'How soon?' he asked.

'Six months. But you'll have to deal with the Whitwell lads before then, Raymond. There are things they will want sorting before we hand over, and Frank isn't up to it.'

Sheila leant across the table and put her hand on Raymond's arm. 'I'm sorry, Raymond, I really am.'

Raymond walked across the yard, past the shippen and over to his caravan. It was a warm evening, the fields were green, the trees behind his caravan full and strong against the sky. Abbeystead had never looked more at peace but Raymond couldn't see it. All he could see was a damp house in a dark town, screeching fat girls and a nasty little man.

Five

It was close to midnight and Ann was stood at the bottom of the back garden, standing where the trees began. Thomas was in his office, drinking, watching tapes of the empty road, making notes about passing neighbours' cars. They hadn't been speaking properly for weeks, months. When they had their first house together he would sometimes join her in the garden and they would stand and look at the night sky together. He would listen to Ann as she pointed out different constellations and planets. Sometimes he wrapped his arms around her and pushed into the back of her, always a sign he wanted to take her to bed, but that wasn't a bad thing. There was even talk of them buying a telescope for a while, a good one, with different lenses and a tripod.

Ann's fascination with space had begun when she was a child. She was born at just the right time; she was eleven years old when man landed on the moon.

Her parents sent her to bed at the usual time but promised to wake her in time to see the landing. She followed her dad downstairs after midnight, dressed in her pyjamas, anticipation quickly replacing her tiredness. She was so excited she was weak; her legs were fizzing, like they could barely support her. She held the banister firmly on her way down the stairs, descending as carefully as she could; she didn't want to fall and die moments before man landed on the moon, that would be a terrible thing to happen. The Tattersalls, their next-door neighbours, had been invited and were sat on the settee where Ann usually sat, so she crawled between her dad's legs and rested her back against the foot of his seat and stared at the television.

'Say hello to Mr and Mrs Tattersall, Ann,' her mum instructed her.

'Hello,' Ann said, glancing their way for a tiny second before returning her unblinking gaze to the television.

'She's not interested in us tonight, Mrs Stead,' said Mr Tattersall. 'Man is about to land on the moon!' He said the words with great exaggeration and winked at Ann, who was staring at the screen as if her neck was fixed forward with rivets.

*

None of it disappointed Ann, not one second. From the sheer blackness of space to the slow-moving man bounding about in his big white suit, it was exactly as she imagined it would be. 'Man on the moon,' she kept saying in her head, 'man is on the moon,' as if repeating the words would help to make the image in front of her understandable somehow. Even now when she looked up at a full white moon she struggled to accept that man had walked there, actually stepped on that rock up there in space. Despite his best intentions Thomas had never really shared her fascination and he eventually stopped joining her in the garden at night. Thomas, Ann discovered, was rooted to what was in front of him – trees, fields and hills impressed him. 'Look at that,' he would say as they drove past Parlick, covered in white frost. 'Spectacular,' he would say at the sight of Coolam Snape being attacked by horizontal rain. Ann wanted to shake him. Abbeystead was just a valley, there were thousands like it and a brief geography lesson could tell you how and when it was formed, whilst up above, if you could be bothered to look, hung a universe. That was exciting to Ann, not a million dark trees gathered together on a wet hillside in the north of England. Ann had read that if you travelled at the speed of light it would take fourteen billion years to cross the universe. And all of that was just above them, right above their heads, but Thomas never looked up. Ann had tried to spark Thomas's interest. She'd told him the sun they were looking at in the middle of the day was a star so big it could contain a million earth-sized planets, and the sun wasn't even a big star, there were bigger, much bigger. Thomas had nodded and said, 'Amazing, isn't it,' but she knew he gave it no real thought, that he didn't find it amazing at all really, that he preferred the cold hard reliability of a north-facing fell.

The night was the one thing about Abbeystead that Ann truly loved. With the nearest city forty miles away there was no light pollution and the night skies could be spectacular. But not tonight. There was heavy cloud cover over the valley and no stars broke through. All around her was black. The lights in the house were off and from the bottom of the garden Ann couldn't see the house at all. She stared so long she began to doubt it actually stood there. She began to shiver. Everything gone; the house, Thomas and the children. The shivering didn't stop. If everything and everyone was gone, there would be nothing left for her to do but turn and walk into the trees.

Six

Keith was taken to an upstairs room by the smiling girl from reception. He was told to help himself to coffee and biscuits, that his interviewer would be along shortly. Keith didn't want anything to eat or drink; he was nervous and sweaty. He'd walked to the interview thinking the exercise would help calm his nerves, but the walk took longer than estimated and he'd ended up rushing and was now hot, sticky and anxious. Keith was surprised at how nervous he was; he was usually blasé about this type of thing. Usually, once he'd got his foot in the door, he was confident about charming people into giving him a chance. This time though he needed the job. He wasn't at the interview to placate Rose, he didn't have any of the money she earned to support him if it didn't go well. And most importantly he needed the job to show Rose how he'd changed when he did, finally, see her again. Keith looked around. The room didn't help with his nerves. He was used to chatting to a man in overalls in a pokey office at the back of a factory, at the side of a warehouse, a radio playing, a calendar of girls on the wall. This place was something else. A thick blue carpet, a large wooden desk, no invoices spilling out of broken files, no stained cups cluttering the place up. On the wall behind the desk hung framed awards and certificates. Keith wandered over to the huge glass window in the far wall and looked down. Men were working away down there, each one of them in EveryFrame overalls, a big white tick on their back. Some were loading up vans with frames, others measuring and cutting glass. Everyone down there busy. Something wasn't right about the scene and Keith couldn't understand what. He only realised when one man called out to another at the far side of the warehouse and the man turned to reply: there was no radio. Whenever Keith had worked in a place like this there had always been a radio blasting out, distorting, sometimes more than one, the songs fighting each other in the air above the workers. What kind of place doesn't have a radio? Keith wondered.

'Busy down there, isn't it,' a voice from behind him said. Keith spun round to see a young woman in a black suit holding a pile of papers. A pair of glasses rested on top of her forehead, pushing back her full dark hair. She was already tall but a steep pair of heels set her even taller. She was young and beautiful and Keith felt short, fat and bald. He walked over to the woman and they shook hands.

Keith said, 'Busy, yes, looks like you're doing well.'

'That's why we're hiring.'

The woman slipped behind the desk and told Keith to have a seat.

'I'm Kerry Pearson, head of HR. I have your CV here,' she patted the paper on the desk in front of her. Keith smiled. He was proud of his CV.

'Before we get into the interview I want to ask about your past experience. You've had lots of different positions.'

Keith smiled again and said, 'I've seen it all.'

'But you've never stayed in one place for long.'

'When I was younger I liked to get out and about, see what I was missing elsewhere. I wanted to see it all and I moved from job to job. But I'm looking for something more stable now.' He laughed a small laugh.

'Was it always your decision to move on?'

Keith nodded firmly. 'I was always keen to try something else. But like I said, I'm after something more permanent now.'

Kerry Pearson didn't say anything. Keith could

feel the sweat surging through his skin like a fever. Should he say more? Had he said enough? Were silences like this usual in this type of interview?

Finally she spoke.

'It's quite an investment for any company to take on and train a new employee. Here we send you on health and safety and first aid courses. We have experienced members of staff take time out from their duties to train new staff. Looking at what's in front of me I'm concerned it wouldn't be worth it. The longest you've stayed in a job is just under a year and that was a long time ago.'

Keith shifted in his seat. Had she not been listening to him? He wanted to joke about having sown his oats and looking to settle down now, but he didn't think the woman in front of him would laugh, or even smile, at a comment like that.

'There are also many gaps here,' she said.

The sweat had worked through to the surface of Keith's skin and he had to wipe his arm across his brow to stop it running into his eyes. He ached. He felt exhausted. The librarian had mentioned the gaps on the CV, saying that employers preferred unbroken employment, but Keith didn't know how to rectify that without making it all up. He'd either walked out, been sacked or was in prison, and he couldn't put any of that down. 'I was looking for work,' he said. 'And looking after the kids. A modern man you see.' Keith smiled but his voice sounded weak and humourless.

'Some of the breaks are for a year or more. There is a section on our application form where it asks if you have a criminal record, if you've ever been convicted of any criminal activity. In my experience it is best to answer this question honestly, Mr Sullivan.'

'No,' Keith said faintly, 'I'm clean.' He didn't know what the matter was. He was normally wonderful at lying.

'Nothing?' she asked. 'Because we go into people's homes. We have to have trustworthy staff.'

Keith shook his head.

'Your last period of employment was at Etherton Cement. Why did you leave there? That's stable work, isn't it? Good money too.'

Keith raised himself in his seat and tried to pull himself together. He looked at the stern young woman across from him and prayed that she would see the man he was trying to become. 'I felt I'd learnt all I could in that position and thought it was time to seek out new opportunities.'

'You parted on good terms?'

'Yes.'

'If we contacted them, they'd be happy to offer us a reference?'

Keith could see his future narrow to a thin slit in front of him. He felt drained of everything. He allowed his vision to become blurred and then closed his eyes. He wanted to sleep. He was so tired.

'Mr Sullivan?' Kerry Pearson said.

With his eyes still closed he asked, 'Why did you ask me to come for an interview? Why did you even bother to have me here?'

'Some of our best workers sent in awful CVs. The men we need here don't always come across well on paper, and, when I can, I like to give people a chance.'

Keith opened his eyes and said, 'But you aren't going to give me a chance, are you?'

Kerry Pearson looked at him and shook her head.

In the pub that night, five pints into a session, Keith remembered who his interviewer had reminded him of. It wasn't only her height – it was the manner of her. Superior, dismissive, controlled and arrogant. He felt the fury inside ramp itself up and then, pop, it was gone. He laughed. He'd had an idea. He finished his pint and ordered another one.

Seven

Raymond lay in his caravan. His meal was going cold on the table in the farmhouse but he wasn't hungry. He was thinking back to a Friday afternoon at school years before. The teacher had asked everyone in the class what they wanted to be when they were older. It was supposed to be a fun way to pass the last half hour of the school week, but like many things that happened at school, it filled Raymond with panic. He knew that if he didn't choose carefully the other boys, and some of the girls, would use his choice to mock him. He was hoping he could steal someone else's dream job, but as the teacher went from child to child he realised their choices were all too grand for him. He couldn't say he wanted to be a footballer, soldier, actor or rock star, his classmates would be offended that thick-lipped Raymond had the arrogance to think he was just the same as the rest of them. When it was eventually his turn to speak all heads turned to face him, waiting for him to claim his future. A few faces were smiling already, primed to laugh, others were glaring, just the sight of him enough to upset some of his classmates. But he still hadn't managed to think of a job that wouldn't draw mockery or anger. He shook his head at the teacher.

'Come on, Raymond,' Mr Tilton said. 'There must be something you want to do. You won't be able to sit daydreaming for the rest of your life.'

Raymond glanced out of the window, looking for inspiration, and it came. Just at that moment a tractor passed on the road, heading out of town, shifting faster than you imagined a tractor could move.

'Farmer,' Raymond said immediately.

Someone laughed, someone else groaned but Raymond felt the tension in the room dissipate and the heads turned away in disappointment. A farmer was perfect. He'd given them nothing to work with; nobody else wanted the job, he wasn't treading on anyone's dream and it was a mundane enough option not to draw ridicule, lowly enough to be accepted as his destiny. The teacher said, 'That will mean long hours and lots of hard work, Raymond. I hope you're prepared.'

And then it was time for the weekend and the class was released. One of Raymond's main aggressors passed him in the corridor and said, 'A farmer, Raymond? You already smell of shit, it should suit you that.' Raymond carried on walking, comments like that hardly registered with him any more.

After that afternoon Raymond had forgotten about the idea of being a farmer until he was sat in Etherton job centre years later, when the man behind the desk spotted his large hands and asked if he'd considered farm work. That was the moment which had led to Raymond sitting on top of Marshaw Fell looking down on Abbeystead, his legs aching from pedalling up the long climb, Etherton miles behind him, not even visible any more. Down below him, the fields and trees, the space, almost empty of people, the land which would become his refuge for years. Lying in his caravan years later Raymond couldn't bear the thought of leaving Abbeystead. He didn't think it would be possible. He didn't think his legs would allow him to walk away.

Eight

Thomas paused the tape and made an entry in his notebook. 15.14, a red Ford Escort, a C reg. The car appeared to slow as it approached the house. Five minutes later the car returned from the opposite direction, but that wasn't unusual, many drivers realised the small road was probably not taking them anywhere in particular and headed back the way they'd come. Thomas stared at the screen, screwing up his eyes and focusing as much as he could, but he couldn't see the driver clearly. He noted that the camera could do with a wipe. He allowed the tape to run on, loosened his tie, undid his collar and stretched. The room was warm, the white flickers of static on the screen rose and fell like slow-leaping digital sheep. He finished his glass of whisky and pushed back in his chair. A minute later his head rocked back, his body went slack and his throat opened, the snores so loud Ann could hear him in the kitchen. He woke half an hour later with a start.

He leant forward and stared at the screen. The static flickered, the road behind it as empty as usual. Thomas stopped the video and put his notebooks away. He straightened the items on his desk, turned off the light and closed the door behind him. He'd been fast asleep when the red Ford Escort returned for a third time and crawled past the house, a pale face inside the car staring intently at the front door.

Nine

Five of them were in the Land Rover, travelling along the Keasden road, heading to the foot of Liverstock Fell. Thomas and Raymond sat in the front, Ann, Daniel and Harriet bumping along together in the back. The walk and the picnic were Ann's idea. A few days before, Raymond had turned up at the house and Thomas had taken him through to the back garden to talk and drink as they usually did. After half an hour Thomas came in to use the toilet and Ann stepped outside to say hello to Raymond. He was sat in one of the garden chairs, his head down, his chin pointing to his massive chest. When Ann approached he looked up. Tears were pouring down his cheeks.

'Raymond, what's the matter?' she asked, crouching down beside him.

Raymond shook his head fiercely and looked away to the bottom of the garden and the trees.

'Sorry,' Ann said, 'I'll leave you,' and walked away,

back into the house, hoping Thomas would hurry back and comfort his friend.

'The farm is being sold and he's losing his job,' Thomas told her later.

'Where will he go?'

'Back to the house in Etherton,' said Thomas. 'He won't be homeless.'

'You said that he hates Etherton. He hates the town and his house.'

'He does. That's why he's so upset.'

'So what did you say to him?'

'What could I say? I don't have a farm, I can't offer him a job.'

The next day Ann decided on the picnic. The best thing to do when something was upsetting you, she believed, was to do anything to keep the mind from dwelling. It was old-fashioned thinking, she knew, but she trusted it. Once the mind was snagged on something, once it got its claws in, it was hard to free it. Ann had seen that with Thomas. And it would do them all good, she decided, to do something together, outside in the fresh air. Harriet had been delighted with the idea, Daniel had moaned, as he moaned about anything that took him away from his computer games, Thomas accepted the plan easily enough and Raymond didn't know how to refuse an invite from Ann, even if he'd wanted to. So there he was, his huge legs taking up all the space in front of him in the Land Rover. Thomas turned on to Demdike Lane and after half a mile pulled into a small, rough car park at the foot of Liverstock Fell. The five of them set off walking up the lower rises of the hill, the gentle climbs before the gradient kicked in. Daniel ran ahead, seemingly not unhappy any more, Harriet skipped around Raymond, and Thomas and Ann brought up the rear. After twenty minutes they reached the foot of the path that ran sharply and diagonally to the top of the fell. The track was steep and narrow and they had to walk in single file and stop regularly for Harriet to catch up. Each time they rested they would turn and look out at the valley spreading below them. Thomas pointed out the gap in the trees of Bleasdale Forest, miles away in the distance, where their house sat, and Raymond pointed out the farmhouse, which could just about be seen. Then he gestured west and told them, 'Sometimes you can see the sea. On a less hazy day there's a shimmer on the horizon and you know it's the sea.'

'What a place,' Thomas said, his hands on his hips, gazing out at Abbeystead.

'It is,' Raymond said.

Ann realised then what she was doing. She was bringing a man who was soon to be exiled from Abbeystead, taking him to the top of the highest point and showing him all of what he was losing. On a beautiful summer's day she was rubbing his nose in it.

'Come on,' she said, briskly, 'let's keep moving.'

They were at the top in an hour. Thomas walked over to a patch of flat grass and said, 'A good spot?'

'Shall we move on a bit?' Ann suggested. She was hoping to pull Raymond away from the view, maybe find somewhere further on which wasn't quite so panoramic.

'I like it here,' Harriet said.

'That settles it then.' Thomas swung the rucksack off his back.

They laid the blanket down on the springy grass, put the flasks and sandwiches in the middle and sat in a line, facing the view.

'It's a lucky dip,' Ann said, pointing to the foil parcels. 'There are tuna, ham, and cheese and pickle. Nobody gets any cake until a whole sandwich is gone.'

They unwrapped their sandwiches, peered inside,

agreed swaps and began to eat. For a few minutes it was quiet as they sat and chewed and gazed down below them. Harriet nuzzled into Thomas and pointed out a range of round-topped hills at the other side of the valley. She yawned and said, 'What are those hills called, Daddy?'

'The pointier one on the left is Parlick, but the others, I get them mixed up. Raymond?'

'Parlick on the left, then Fairsnape, then Saddle Fell and that over there is Clougha Pike,' Raymond said, pointing as he went.

'There are supposed to be witches over there, they told us at school,' Harriet said.

Thomas and Ann laughed, but Raymond said, 'Back in the seventeenth century. They were tried in court for it, about ten women.'

'But they weren't really witches, were they?' Ann asked.

Raymond shrugged. 'Some said they were. Some say it's because they were Catholic. I don't know too much about it, but Sheila was telling me one night, she says she's related to those who were on trial.'

Thomas put his arm around Harriet. 'Maybe, when it's dark, Harriet, we could walk up into those hills, see if we can see ourselves a witch?'

'No way,' Harriet said, shuddering and pushing

herself even closer to her dad. 'Not in the dark.'

'You weren't scared of the dark when you were little, not at all.'

'Wasn't I?' Harriet asked.

'When you were a baby you would cry at night, all night sometimes. You would scream and scream so I would put you in the car and drive around, to see if I could get you off to sleep. That was how we ended up living here, that was how I found the barn. On some nights I would park the car and walk into the forest with you in the middle of the night. You never cried in the forest. I would walk through the trees with you, sit down against a tree and hold you, wondering what it was about the forest that soothed you.' Thomas stroked Harriet's hair. 'And look at you now. You hardly cry at anything.'

Raymond's jaw had frozen mid chew. All those years and he'd never realised. That night in the forest, the only people he'd ever seen on his midnight walks and it had been Thomas and Harriet. Of course it had been Thomas and Harriet. Sat with the Nortons on top of Liverstock Fell, with a sandwich in one hand, a plastic cup of coffee in the other, Abbeystead below, Raymond was flummoxed. He'd never been happier or sadder in his life.

Ten

Two weeks after the walk Thomas was sitting in the pale green room at the back of Maltham health centre. Opposite him was Dr Barbour.

'How are the children?' she asked.

'They are fine, thank you, I think.'

'And how is Ann?'

Ann. She must have made notes after they'd left. He wondered what she'd written about him.

'She's fine too.' Thomas scratched his head. 'Well, she is fine but she's annoyed with me.'

'Why is she annoyed with you, Thomas?'

Thomas paused. At home, with the trees surrounding the house and the knowledge that the nearest human being who could offer help was at least two miles away, his behaviour, his worry, seemed perfectly sensible, common sense in fact. Here, he wasn't so sure. He didn't want to tell this woman he made notes from security cameras about every passing car. He didn't want to say he set traps in the trees and checked them daily for human disturbance. When he thought about those things spoken out loud he pictured a mad man with a beard, long greasy hair and dirty fingernails.

'I've not been myself,' he said. 'I'm not sleeping well, I might be drinking too much. I'm anxious a lot of the time. I snap at the kids, and Ann. I find it hard to get up, to start the day.'

'How long have you been like this?'

'Ever since it happened. Well, as soon as the shock disappeared and the reality of it set in.'

'It's been months, what spurred you to come and see me now?'

'It will sound stupid,' Thomas said.

Dr Barbour shook her head. 'Nothing you say in this room is considered stupid, Thomas.'

'We went for a walk and I felt better.' Thomas shrugged. 'For a bit, for a few hours anyway. We went for a picnic the other day, with a friend, and for the first time in a long time I wasn't thinking about what had happened and whether the men would come back. Even on the drive home I wasn't wondering if the men would be waiting. It didn't last all day, just when we were walking and an hour or so afterwards. But I remembered what it felt like to feel normal again. I've been lost to that feeling.'

He stopped talking.

'And you want to feel like that more of the time?'

'I don't know if I can. But it was almost better when I didn't realise how bad I had been feeling. Then it seemed impossible to feel anything else; it was just how it was. But I felt normal for a few hours, or for moments within those hours, and . . .' Thomas ran out of steam. 'Well, yes, I want to feel like that more of the time.'

'Have you seen your doctor?' Dr Barbour asked.

Thomas shook his head.

'So you aren't on any medication?'

'No,' Thomas said, 'nothing.'

'How would you feel about that? Something to help with anxiety and depression? We will try other techniques alongside, but it can help to kick-start things.'

'I'm not depressed,' Thomas said.

'Perhaps not. We will see. It's my job to diagnose you.'

Thomas shook his head. He was sure he wasn't depressed. It wasn't fair or accurate to call what he was going through depression. He didn't have any say in what had happened to him, the position he now found himself in. He didn't wake up one morning and suddenly see the world as dark and inhospitable.

This had been thrust on him. And he wasn't sure about medication. He didn't want to be a man who took pills for his nerves. It sounded like something that would happen to a friend of his mother's, something she would whisper about conspiratorially over Sunday lunch.

'You say you've been drinking more?' Dr Barbour asked.

'It's crept up,' said Thomas. 'It takes the edge off things.'

'Well that's a form of self-medication, and neither the safest or the healthiest. If we do think medication would be beneficial we can monitor any side effects, tweak the dose, try a different course of pills. Alcohol isn't a good idea. In the short term you might think it's helping but over time it only makes anxiety and depression worse. But we're getting ahead of ourselves. For now tell me how you've been feeling. Describe how you feel from morning to night on an average day.'

Depression. She'd used that word again. Pushing his resentment aside Thomas took a deep breath and began. He explained how he woke tired from lack of sleep because he couldn't sleep with the thought of the men in the trees, waiting to strike again. And because he was tired, and probably hungover, he was short with Ann and the kids in the morning. But that was once he got himself out of bed. Sometimes, just to achieve that simple feat, it felt like he had to build himself, brick by brick from the bottom to the top and then lift his body, like a crane lifting a boulder, from the bed. Work was something to be got through. He phoned home several times a day to check that Ann was alright, but he wasn't nice to her, he didn't want to chat. He just wanted to know the men hadn't returned and then he would hang up. When Ann rang him he always presumed the worst, his heart would pound, his hands shake, and he would react badly if she wanted him to pick up bread or milk. You rang me for that . . . The drive home, the drive he used to love, out of town and up on to the wide hills, the journey he used to find so thrilling was now excruciating, every second shot through with worry. He was certain he was returning home to a family held at gunpoint. And then, when that hadn't materialised for another day, he would sit and brood and fret in his office, insisting on silence, wondering when the men would strike again. The children he loved, he was desperate to protect them, but he found them a nuisance now. He didn't want to be playing a silly game with them when he should be on guard. He didn't like their noise and the chaos they brought to the house. It was harder to hear anyone approach when they were playing games, shouting up and down the stairs, chasing around. Every day had become about survival. He didn't look forward to, or enjoy, anything about his life any more. Everything good had been replaced by fear. Thomas finished talking and looked at Dr Barbour with an expression of embarrassment and hopelessness.

She smiled kindly at him, scribbled a note, and it was all Thomas could do not to burst into tears.

'We will talk about your reaction to what happened and how you can manage it in the coming weeks, but initially I want to set you a small exercise. What I'm going to suggest might sound silly; it might seem like I'm giving you a canoe to cross an ocean, but I want you to go with it. Each day I want you to record a few things. When you wake up I want you to write down a number from one to ten, reflecting how you are feeling about the day ahead. Ten is raring to go, happy with the world and your place in it, can't wait to get out and get on with your day. One is anxious, full of dread, can't get out of bed, a feeling of total hopelessness. And before you go to bed in the evening I want you to score how the day actually was. When you've got through the day, score it again out of ten, a number representing how the day was in reality. And finally, but importantly, I want you to write down three positive things that happen every day. Three good things that happened to you.'

Thomas looked at Dr Barbour. 'Three good things that happen every day?' he asked.

'Yes. They don't have to be huge things – my daughter smiled at me, the sun shone, I had my favourite sandwich for lunch, whatever you can find, anything you can find. But three of them, and every day. Write them down and bring your notes to the next session.'

With his homework set a sceptical Thomas drove home. The fear inside him hadn't lessened a dot, the blackness he saw everywhere was still as complete. As the car entered the forest Thomas thought that maybe Dr Barbour was right, maybe this was depression.

Eleven

They were sad days on the farm for Raymond, but the work had a way of getting in the way of the sadness and sometimes Raymond was able to forget he was on his final stretch in Abbeystead. The middle Whitwell brother came over one sunny Tuesday morning, but he didn't seem to expect anything from Raymond and he didn't have any work he wanted doing before his family took over the running of the farm. Raymond wasn't sure why he was there, didn't know what to do with him, so he walked him around the farm and showed him where everything was, explained what jobs he did when, but Whitwell didn't seem interested; didn't say much and only looked to be half listening. His one concern appeared to be the date Raymond would be finishing.

'So you finish on the fourth, we come in on the fifth,' he said, more than once, and Raymond nodded that he understood that to be the case. Just before he left Whitwell turned to Raymond and said, 'The caravan, Raymond, Frank's asked if we'll get rid of it when we start. He wants it gone.' Raymond felt a surge of anger. Didn't they understand he realised he was finished at the farm? 'I finish on the fourth, you start on the fifth. Do what you like with the caravan,' he said, and stalked off, leaving Whitwell standing in the middle of the yard. It was the only time in his life Raymond had been intentionally rude to anyone.

On the nights Raymond wasn't at the Nortons' he spent his evenings walking. It was June and the sun was in the sky until after nine and Raymond took advantage. He crossed the valley after tea, walking through every field he could find, exploring every copse, crossing every stream. He didn't care whose fields he was walking through or who saw him. Let them see him, let them talk. He was going to get as much of Abbeystead for himself before it was too late. These walks were different from his night walks; they weren't to exhaust him, to convince his body to allow him to sleep. He was hungry for Abbeystead, for every inch of it, and he kept his eyes wide open, taking it in, every tree, every hillock, every stone wall. He wanted to see it, to record it, so he could remember at will when he was back in the house in

Etherton and it seemed impossible that such a place as this existed.

'Have you thought about getting out there? Asking around? Seeing if anybody else in the valley needs help?' Thomas had asked him. But Raymond knew that was hopeless. Every farmer in Abbeystead would know about the Whitwell deal, they probably knew about it before he did. He was cheap and good, the work would have been offered if it was there. And anyway, what was the likelihood he would find a farmer who was happy to have him living in all the time? Maybe he could pick up a few days' work, but not enough to save him from Etherton. There was nothing for him other than to move back to his house. What would come after that, he didn't know. Standing at the bottom of Wennington waterfall, underneath the trees on the bank, with the cold water flooding down the drop, crashing into the pool in an angry mess, Raymond looked up to the lip of the waterfall. It was a drop, but maybe not far enough. And who was to say he wouldn't miss the brutal rocks, land in the deep water and be carried safely to the shore anyway. That would be just his clumsy luck.

Twelve

On the first morning of emotion scoring Thomas sat on the edge of the bed and considered what number most closely reflected his feelings about the day ahead of him. He felt horrible, was the truth. A bad back, a stiff neck and the usual dose of anxiety. What he wanted most was to be able to crawl back into bed and sleep for another five hours. But, on the other hand, he wasn't dying, he wasn't in extreme pain, the children and Ann were safe in the kitchen. Thomas opened his notebook and wrote down a four in the first column. The moment he lifted the pen from the paper a scream rang out from downstairs. Thomas shot to his feet, but then he could hear Ann telling Harriet not to be so silly, a spider was nothing to be scared of. Thomas sat back down, crossed out the four and replaced it with a two. Each morning was awarded a two after that.

Thomas normally enjoyed filling columns with

figures, but he was used to dealing with numbers which had been checked and double-checked, figures which couldn't be questioned. Here he was entering made-up numbers about his own shifting feelings. And who was he to say if his misery was currently at one or three? Maybe he thought he was at one but there were further depths to fall which he hadn't experienced yet. This guesswork reminded him of A level English literature. In physics and maths he learnt the formulas and rules, applied them to the questions and sailed through the classes and exams. If he got an answer wrong it was explained to him where he went wrong and he rarely made the same mistake again. English lit wasn't as straightforward. He wasn't as confident as some students who would swoop on a black door in a poem and award it layers of symbolism and meaning, seemingly at will from their own imaginations. Thomas wasn't happy guessing what the poet might have been saying with the choice of a black door. And as he heard his classmates suggest the door symbolised death, depression, darkness, fear, Thomas wanted to say that perhaps the black door didn't symbolise anything gloomy or threatening for the poet at all. Maybe the poet had good memories of a black door from his childhood; maybe the black door was the front door of his loving grandparents' house. But he didn't have the confidence to say anything at all. It was the uncertainty that unsettled Thomas. He preferred to answer a question with an answer he knew to be correct, his working on the paper evidence that he understood.

By the end of the fourth day Thomas thought he was beginning to understand the point of the exercise. In the morning, with the threat of another day in front of him, his score would invariably be a point or two below his score in the evening, when the day had been survived without anything diabolical happening. He still didn't score any day higher than a five, although in truth a couple of days should have been sixes and one night, when Thomas and Ann had made love for the first time in a long time, he could have even gone as high as a seven, but he kept his scores at steady fives, to make sure Dr Barbour's point wasn't made too easily.

Initially he found the 'three positives' task tricky. He scrabbled for anything on the first few days and was forced to steal a couple of Dr Barbour's suggestions – Harriet smiled at me, Lovely evening meal – even when those things hadn't happened. But as the days wore on he found it easier to come up with positives and some days he ended up having to choose which ones to use and he even held some over in reserve for a bad day. It became easier, Thomas believed, because he was on the lookout for positives. So when he met his colleagues in the morning he would notice if anyone greeted him warmly; he was watching as he walked through Maltham to see if there was an acquaintance offering him a wave from the other side of the street. The weather and Abbeystead made frequent appearances in his three positives. With it being June there was so much light, so much beauty every day on his drives to and from work. Again, Thomas understood the point of the exercise – to encourage the mind to look for the positives every day, and whilst he was sure that such simple tricks could not affect the darkness of the moods he'd been carrying he recorded his numbers, and searched for, and wrote down, his three positives every day.

Thirteen

Keith had given up not drinking. He'd given up fruit. He'd given up on Rose. For the first time in his life he'd abandoned his appearance. His remaining hair was greasy and long, trailing damply from his scalp over his collar. His clothes weren't washed or ironed and they hung from him in musty clumps. Rose had rarely spoken about Keith to her friends, but she would tell them, 'He knows his way around a washing machine. He can iron a shirt so it will cut you.' The truth was Keith never washed Rose's clothes or the girls', just his own, and he only learnt to wash and iron because he was unhappy with Rose shrinking his trousers, running the colours, not bothering to iron the collars and cuffs of his shirts, like his mum had. Keith, despite everything else, had always looked smart. But now, most days, he didn't clean his teeth.

Keith had been a positive man. He'd always imagined that one day he would get to where he deserved to be. Even when he was in prison his optimism hadn't abandoned him. For a man like him, a man who was going to tread his own path, prison was a risk. But no matter how bad it had been in the past it seemed evident to Keith that as a king wears a crown, so he would, one day, be wealthy and free. He'd always seen himself, in the future (it was never the distant future, at most two or three years ahead), striding through streets in expensive clothes with a beautiful woman on his arm and money in his pocket. And for a few months, his wallet stuffed heavy with cash, it felt like he'd finally been on his way. And then, how quickly he'd become a man in dirty clothes, in a filthy house, fatness weighing him down.

Keith blamed women.

He blamed his mother for being so short, for not finding a taller husband, for loving him so much he didn't realise there was anything different about him until he heard a teacher at school describe him as 'the short one, the little lad'. He blamed Rose for being as poor as him, for not having money for both of them, for not wanting the life he wanted and for expecting him to be a dull, average, everyday working man. He blamed the young woman at EveryFrame who taunted him with an interview. A beautiful woman with the looks of a film star, almost a foot taller than him, everything in the world could be hers and he had nothing and all he needed from her was a 'yes' but she'd shaken her head. He blamed tall women who never even registered his presence. Stalking around on long legs, marrying tall men, giving birth to even taller children – the tall women of the world gradually shrinking Keith away to nothing. But his anger often returned to one woman. A rich woman in a beautiful house, a woman he'd held hostage for twelve hours and who'd barely flinched. He'd touched her little girl on the head and spoken some kind words. 'Don't you fucking touch her,' he'd been told.

When Keith's anger threatened to overwhelm him, he allowed himself to remember his plan. It helped calm him. And whilst Keith didn't see himself waltzing along with beautiful women any more, he certainly didn't intend to live in his own dirt in Etherton for the rest of his life. He was going to allow himself a few more days in this state, then he would see.

Fourteen

'Thomas, every time we've met you've appeared tense, agitated at times. You sit in the chair with your shoulders hunched and you lean forward as if anticipating an attack.'

Thomas sat up in his chair, pushed his shoulders back and Dr Barbour laughed.

'It's something we should look at, particularly if you are intent on avoiding medication. I want you to learn to relax. If the body is tense the mind is tense too, wondering what has alarmed the body, wondering why the body is on guard. The mind begins to anticipate threat, which means the body tenses even more, and the mind becomes more distraught.'

Thomas shifted in his seat and instructed his body to relax but his tendons were metal brackets drilled into the concrete slabs of his muscles.

'Stress is a powerful thing,' Dr Barbour continued. 'It works into our bodies and is difficult to get rid of once it's there. It means we are constantly in a fight-

or-flight state, always ready to do battle or run, and that is bad for health, physical and mental.'

Thomas knew that to be the case. It was exhausting to be on edge all the time, jumping every time one of the children dropped something to the floor, feeling the kick of fear when the phone rang or a door slammed.

'What I'm going to suggest might seem unusual, some people don't expect to hear this type of advice in a clinical setting, but there is evidence to show that there are benefits and with some clients it has worked very well, so I want you to at least consider it.'

'Consider what?' Thomas asked.

'Meditation, Thomas.'

Thomas shook his head.

'You don't think it could help you?' Dr Barbour asked.

'I'm sure it works for some people, but I doubt it's for me. It's doing nothing essentially, isn't it? Zoning out? I like to be doing something; I find it hard to do nothing. That's why I used to walk, that was how I relaxed, by being active.'

'But you don't walk now, do you? Because you don't like to leave the house when the family are at home, so we need to find you something that will help with your anxiety and stress, something you can do at home. And you are quite wrong in your understanding of meditation – it is the opposite of zoning out. Meditation is about focus, it isn't about being distant and unaware; it's about being completely aware. To meditate successfully you have to be present in the activity, present in the world.'

Dr Barbour shifted in her chair. 'Are you ever involved in a task so completely that you are lost in it, Thomas? Your body and mind are working together, you aren't thinking about what to eat that night, you aren't worried if you are saving enough for your pension, you aren't worried about how the children are doing at school or thinking about a row you had with Ann. You are involved and absorbed by the task in hand. You feel calm, engaged and in control?'

Thomas thought he understood. He nodded.

'Well that is what meditation is, in a way. It's about that kind of focus, that absorption. But rather than getting that satisfaction through work we get to it by meditation. Our body learns to relax, our mind learns to focus; we become aware of living in the moment, being present in the moment. The exercise I asked you to do, finding three positives every day – has that helped at all?'

'It's too early to say,' Thomas said.

'Keep it up. The way it works is by dragging your thoughts away from what has become their default setting of worry and stress and focusing on the things that are actually in front of you. So whilst your thoughts are trying to burrow deeper into darkness and anxiety, you've been pulling them up by their roots and saying, "But look at this, now, in front of me. This is a good thing. I can see it and I'm making a note of it." By doing that every day, by looking for and noticing the positives, you are reprogramming your brain. Meditation can help with that. At the moment your brain is constantly dreading what might happen in the future, is it not? You are worrying almost every second about what happened in the past and what might happen next, yes?'

'Yes,' said Thomas, 'it feels exactly like that.'

'What meditation can do is strip that away. It places you in the present, it involves you in the day and anchors you in reality. It can tear you away from the worry storms in your head.'

Dr Barbour leant forward to take a drink from her glass of water.

Thomas looked at the neat woman in front of him and felt angry. Had her house been invaded? Had she worried about the safety of her family for twelve hours? Had the person she loved been attacked? He'd come to her for help and she'd had him writing lists and numbers and now her next suggestion was meditation. A resistance inside him broke.

'But it can't change what happened, can it?' Thomas said before Dr Barbour had the chance to start talking again. 'And it can't change what might happen in the future. Me meditating isn't going to stop men coming into my house with guns. They burst in and find me sitting with my legs crossed, bloody humming. What good is that to anyone?'

He'd spoken with feeling and was embarrassed, but Dr Barbour didn't look slighted or surprised.

'We come back to this, Thomas, what could happen, over and over, and what I'm trying to make clear is that we don't have control over many things. You are right – a frightening thing happened and could happen again to you and your family, and there might be nothing you can do about it. Car crash, cancer, mugging, rape, murder, all of these things happen to someone, somewhere, every day. And the brutal truth is everyone we love is going to die and there is nothing we can do about it. But is that what you want to spend the rest of your life focused on? The terrible, black, sickening aspects of life? Or would you rather take control where you can and stop wasting all of your energy on the things you can't affect? What we can have some control over, if we try, is how we are living now. So you aren't constantly worried about what might, or could, happen, because you are engaged with the present. You are living now.'

Dr Barbour looked at Thomas intently. 'You are only ever alive now, Thomas. No matter who you are, where you are or what you are doing, you are only ever alive now. Right now you are in this room with me and right now there is no catastrophe. Do you want to waste all those "nows" feeling haunted, stressed and worried?'

She stopped speaking. There was an angle of uplift to her chin. Thomas didn't respond.

'Meditation', she continued, calmer in tone, 'helps you to live moment by moment, and in that way, hopefully, you will be less plagued by the future or the past. But what I want you to understand, Thomas, is that meditation is a practical tool. It's not some wishy-washy escape into half-thought-out mysticism, it's about getting closer to reality.'

She looked around the room and her eyes fell on the water in front of her. She picked up the glass and held it up. 'Meditation is as useful and functional as the glass that is holding this water.'

Thomas looked at her, holding the glass aloft.

'You don't happen to meditate yourself, do you, Dr Barbour?' he asked.

'What makes you think that?' she said, smiling and carefully lowering the glass to the table.

Fifteen

Ann returned from taking the children to school and her visit into town. She stepped out from the car and looked up to the blue sky. It was still early but already there was warmth in the day. She leant back as far as she could and let the sun work on her skin. Half an hour before, Ann had spoken to Conner Ryan, the first time she'd seen him in more than ten years. A man had stepped out of a shop in front of her and Ann hadn't given him a second glance, would never have recognised him if he hadn't turned as she passed and said, 'Ann?' She stopped and looked at the man. When she lingered over the mouth and eyes a spark fired in the far corner of her memory but it didn't lead her anywhere conclusive.

'Conner,' he said, finally.

'Conner!' Ann said, not believing, still looking for more clues. 'How are you?'

Ann drove home slowly, hardly bothering to change

gear. She'd thought of Conner over the years and occasionally let her imagination consider other paths her life could have taken. In these imaginings she was poor and living with Conner in a tiny house, no children. He was still riding his motorbike, still as ridiculously handsome and as energetic and exciting as he always had been. In Ann's imaginings they lived a busy life without responsibility. But the man stood in front of her didn't look busy or excited, and even as he was talking, confirming who he was, Ann couldn't accept it was Conner. Not Conner Ryan. There were no remnants of his looks left. His stomach burst out from under his ribcage as pronounced as a beach ball. His hair, which had always been falling forward into his eyes or ruffling its way over his collar, was shaved to the bone of a bumpy, red skull. And his face, the face that had made her laugh with shock at its beauty the first time she saw it, was swollen, the ruthless cheekbones buried under bloated flesh. None of this should matter of course, Ann was thinking as she tried to disguise her shock at the state of him, but it did matter. It was tragic. This was the man every woman in Maltham had wanted. The man who drew women to the pub when he was working, who could choose any woman in the town, any woman in the north of the country probably. The man who tore around on his orange and black motorbike, breaking hearts and then refusing to talk. Ann wanted to ask Conner if he missed his looks – if he was aware of how beautiful he had been, how adored he was back then. Instead they spoke about their children, smiled at each other, said it was nice to see one another, and parted. Ann walked away thinking: that was Conner Ryan? That was Conner Ryan? The beautiful young man who'd broken her heart, who'd set her on the course of the rest of her life, was a lost-looking man holding a plastic bag, wearing a pair of jeans and a baggy T-shirt.

Ann closed the car door. The trees rustled noisily as if they were being shaken at their roots and a warm breeze ran over her body. She arched her back again and pushed herself up, closer to the sun. Life is impossible, she thought, and was suddenly filled with hard, uncomplicated joy. She sensed tears coming, good tears, but she pushed them away and laughed instead, focusing on the happiness she felt. The happiness was real, like a material injected into her and she wanted to savour it. She looked at the house, the house that had refused to welcome her, the house where they had been invaded by men in masks, where she had been punched and the children terrified. The house where she lived with maddening, infuriating Thomas. The house that was, for no reason Ann could understand, finally beginning to feel like home. Life was impossible. She gathered her bags and walked to the front door, her legs steady and strong underneath her. This was living, she thought, the dark and the glory. Sometimes together. Ann smiled at the wickedness of it. It was then she decided – Thomas's birthday was approaching. They were going to have a party.

Sixteen

Thomas drove to Raymond's caravan. Ann was preparing for the party and demanded he remove himself and not return before six. He still hated leaving Ann and the children at the house, but he didn't want to be accused of ruining the party before it began. He tried to remember Dr Barbour's advice: catastrophes happen very rarely, live in the present, focus on the now, but when he passed a battered white van heading in the direction of the house, all Thomas wanted to do was turn and follow. He made himself continue to Raymond's, hating the easy certitude of the woman who'd never been held hostage. He collected Raymond and they drove to the foot of Parlick. As they began the climb he said to Raymond, 'You don't mind this party, do you? I know it's not come at the best time.'

Raymond shook his head. 'But I haven't had chance to pick up a present, I'm sorry.'

Thomas laughed. 'I'm too old for presents, Raymond. I can't think of a single thing I want anyway.'

They walked slowly and spoke little. They stopped when they reached a wooden gate in a stone wall and turned and looked behind them, at how far they'd come. In the distance the southern fells of Abbeystead ran in a proud line, fencing the valley in.

'I don't know what it is about hills,' Thomas said. 'I've always liked hills, climbing up them, walking down them, even just looking at them. I've no idea why, but I could look at them for hours. Somebody should write something about the psychology of hills, if they haven't already.'

He laughed at his words, but they brought back a memory from childhood.

'I went on holiday with my mum and dad when I was about ten. We went to Suffolk and I'd never seen anything like it. I knew it would be flat, they'd told me that, but it was just so eerie, for a lad used to hill country. I didn't understand how you were supposed to know where you were – there were no landmarks, nothing to gauge your progress by. We were staying in this cottage down a track with a huge back garden and I climbed a tree to see if anything was out there, but it was just endless fields to the horizon. It sounds silly but I became panicky. It seemed to me the kind of countryside that would exist after a nuclear war –

faceless and flat – nothing remaining. You could see the sun go right down behind the low horizon, like it was dropping away and never coming back. When my parents sensed there was something wrong I told them I felt unwell, but really I was terrified that the world was ending. I wanted to get home to check that the hills were still there, to check that the whole world hadn't been flattened down.'

'I've never been anywhere without hills,' Raymond said. 'I find it hard to imagine.'

Thomas leant into the wall and said, 'But I suppose people who grow up in flat places find it unusual to be confronted by hills and fells at every turn. That's probably as strange to them as the flatness is to us.'

'I don't think anyone could ever find Abbeystead strange,' Raymond replied. 'It seems the most natural place on the planet to me. The first time I saw it, I thought – there it is, that's what you've been looking for.'

Raymond looked unbearably sad and Thomas was grateful when a strong gust of wind blew in and prompted them to walk on. They turned their backs on the view and kept moving slowly up the climb.

Seventeen

Keith had been drinking in Etherton from eleven. He went to the quieter pubs on the edge of town where he could drink alone in neglected corners and gather himself. He'd been drinking heavily for days and felt ill, but despite this he looked back at his recent sobriety through the eyes of a disbeliever. He couldn't understand what he thought he was doing then, who that person was. Keith knew that whatever happened from now on, he would always be a drinker. At two, weary and drunk, he went home to sleep. After a rest he would get on with it, he would climb into the car and drive out to the posh country house. Then he could think about finding Rose. But first he needed sleep. He dropped into bed and slept a black sleep. He woke a couple of hours later feeling worse than ever. Pains in his neck shot into his jaw and he was still exhausted. He decided then that he wouldn't go; he would have to wait a little longer for the money. But he began to shiver. Why was he so cold? It was summer and he was freezing. At least the car would be warm, he thought. He would crank up the heater and drive out to the country. Then, if he felt up to it, he would do it.

Eighteen

Ann prepared for the party. Harriet wanted to help, she always wanted to help, but Ann needed to work quickly, so she encouraged her to watch a favourite film, and now she was sat on the couch with knees up in front of her, cushion grasped tightly, thumb in mouth. Daniel was, of course, in his room, probably having already forgotten they were having a party. Ann made sandwiches, poured crisps into bowls, pulled drinks and glasses from cupboards and arranged them on the table. She quickly tidied the house and pinned banners up.

Happy Birthday! was stuck to the banister, *It's your Birthday!* to the kitchen wall, *Time to Party!* went up in the front room.

Ann smiled when she shoved the pins into that one. She was sure Thomas didn't think it was time to party. She blew up the balloons sitting on the couch with Harriet, watching a few minutes of a film she'd seen hundreds of times before. When the balloons were inflated and tied Ann walked with them bouncing around her and opened the front door to tie them to the handle. Before she had a chance to begin the knot she noticed a small man walking slowly across the lane towards her, he looked lost. Ann turned to greet him. She laughed as the balloons bobbled around her, obscuring her view. She pulled them to one side and said, 'Hello?'

The man stared at Ann and then at the balloons and frowned.

'Are you lost?' Ann asked.

'I've got a knife,' the man said, quietly.

'I'm sorry,' Ann said. 'What did you say?'

The man was sweating. He looked like he might be sick. He gripped himself and crouched down. Ann stepped forward.

'Are you alright?' she asked. 'Do you want some water?'

The man shook his head.

'I think you need to sit down,' Ann said, and the man dropped with a thump to the doorstep. Ann rushed to the kitchen, letting the balloons go in the hallway. She filled a glass with water. Should she call an ambulance? she wondered. She was still considering if this would be an overreaction when she returned to the front door with the water. Stepping outside she heard a car approach. It was their car, Thomas had returned early, that was good – they could decide what to do together. Ann handed the glass of water to the slumped figure, but he shook his head. He was staring at the car and Thomas, who was clambering out as quickly as he could.

'Who's this?' Thomas asked, striding forward. 'What's going on?' Alarm was ratcheted across his face and Ann was immediately annoyed. He always had to look for disaster.

'He's lost, I think. But he's not very well.'

Raymond was out of the car too now. 'Why are you here?' he asked the sitting figure.

The man pulled himself up and stared at Raymond.

'I've got a knife,' he said, almost shouting it this time.

The words spread out around them and into the trees. Nobody moved from where they were stood. The silence reached its pinnacle and then Harriet stepped out from behind Ann and said, 'Why is everyone out here?'

The man moved his hand to his pocket and Raymond charged at him.

The little man shot across the road and burst into

the trees. Behind him, as quickly as he could propel his large body, followed Raymond.

Keith had no idea where he was heading and didn't feel well enough to run, but once he was up and off he moved quickly. He'd forgotten how fast his legs could work. He tore through the trees, jumping over streams, ripping through bushes, pushing himself as hard as he could. He heard the clumsy giant, grunting and thrashing, as threatening as a chasing earthquake. Keith wondered how long he could keep ahead of those massive legs, but then he heard a cry of pain and looked over his shoulder to see his neighbour crash to the forest floor. He felt the sweet kick of victory. His robbery attempt was a disaster, Rose was gone and never coming back, he was fat, ill and broke, but he'd outrun the gormless giant from next door. Keith didn't slow; he pushed himself harder in celebration. He would get to his car and drive for miles. Keith felt joy at this realisation. He could just go. There was a world where people didn't know who he was, what he'd done, how he'd failed. There were thousands of places he could go. All those towns and cities. All that opportunity. Keith skipped elegantly over a fallen branch and smiled. There were people worse off than him, there always would be.

He still had his spirit. His verve. Ahead he saw the track leading to his car. A new path, he thought, that was all he needed. Keith stopped and looked around, making sure nobody was following. Why the fuck would someone live all the way out here? he wondered. Particularly if you had all that money? Why wouldn't you choose to be somewhere there was some life? Some pubs? Keith's new home would have to be close to a good pub, that was a certainty. He set off walking again but only moved forward two steps before he was brought to a halt. It felt like an aeroplane was landing on his chest. He tried to suck in air but air refused to be drawn. His body was crushing itself from the inside. Keith felt more pain than he'd felt in his life, but only briefly. He fell to his knees, rocked forward onto his head and dropped to his side. He was almost dead before he knew he was dying, but not quite. Keith experienced moments of terror as he realised what was happening to him, alone in a forest, in the middle of nowhere. Then he lay there, dead on the forest floor, like a shrew frozen in a frost.

Nineteen

Thomas's eyes itched and he felt sick. He was in the kitchen in Abbeystead, but he needed to be somewhere else. He pored over the map in front of him. Thurso, Lairg, Lochinver, Tongue. Those places (were they towns? Villages even?) must be at least four hundred miles away. His eyes scoured the map of the Highlands – a few thin roads but mainly empty. Open country. The kind of landscape you would see a man coming. Thomas needed clear ground around him, he needed to be able to see what was coming next.

He phoned his boss. 'They came back,' he said. 'Back to the house. I'm going away for a few days, with the family.'

He hung up before more talk was needed, before questions were asked. The company, his boss, his colleagues, had all been helpful, kind and understanding. It was the bank who paid for the security camera and nobody questioned the time Thomas had taken off. And they hadn't questioned his work either, or lack of it. It was impossible sometimes for Thomas to concentrate, to muster any focus to complete even the simplest tasks. Some days he did nothing but close his office door and avoid everyone for as long as possible. Work had been patient but Thomas sensed they were looking to draw a line. They wanted efficient, punctual, clean and sober Thomas back. Maybe empty Scotland would help him return to himself, he thought, without believing it really could, as he called the children's school and pulled the children out, ignoring the concerns of the head teacher, hardly listening to her. He noted Ann, watching him warily, as he made these calls, but she didn't say anything, didn't intervene. At the travel agent's Thomas scanned the list of available houses and booked the first free cottage in an acceptable spot. The blonde woman in the red jacket behind the computer tried to dissuade him.

'It's not really a family holiday home, that one,' she warned him. 'It's not close to anywhere, it's normally rented out to fishermen. And it's very basic, just somewhere for them to sleep at the end of a day's fishing.'

Thomas looked at the map in front of him again.

He saw how far away the cottage sat from where he currently was and said, 'Book it.'

Returning home he ordered the family to pack.

'We'll need to do a food shop, Thomas,' Ann told him. 'We'll need provisions.'

'We'll pick them up on the way,' Thomas said.

Ann packed and then helped the children with their clothes. Daniel and Harriet, unfazed by the idea of this sudden holiday, happily pulled clothes out of drawers and threw them onto beds.

Thomas insisted they set off that afternoon; he was desperate to put some distance between himself and Abbeystead. He didn't drive recklessly, but he drove quickly, barely moving out of the third lane. Other motorists sensed the vehicle surging behind them contained a determined man and moved out of his way. After the excited chatter from the children for the first couple of hours they grew quiet. Ann fell asleep, Daniel stared out of the window and Harriet lost herself in one of her books. Thomas used the peace to scan his body for tension. He was waiting for the hunted feeling to disappear. Surely, he thought, as he passed into Scotland, and then through the lowlands, and further on, higher up, single-lane roads only, mountains on his left and in front of him, he would start to feel safe soon. He looked at the dashboard: 350 miles he'd put between them and the house. How many miles would be enough? He still felt as threatened as when he was sat in his lounge with a line of masked men against the wall.

They arrived at the house in Highland black; they could barely see the building at all. Thomas was exhausted and it took him all his strength to climb out of the car and walk the few yards to the front door. He found the key where he was told it would be, underneath the third stone to the left of the front door, and let the family in. The cottage was basic. A small kitchen, a lounge with a tiny TV, a row of old paperback books on a mahogany dresser, two bedrooms and a simple bathroom, all on one floor. The carpets were dark and swirling, the decor cheap and dated throughout. He could sense the disappointment leaking from the children; this wasn't the type of holiday they were used to. And when they realised they had to share a room Daniel became angry. 'She breathes too noisily when she sleeps and I can hear her sucking her thumb in the night. It makes me sick. I'm eleven years old. I need my own room.'

Thomas couldn't hear this. Not now. He looked at

Daniel and said, in a steady, low voice, 'Shut up. You'd better shut up now.'

Daniel looked at Thomas, searching for the joke, but there was no crack of a smile, no compassion evident, and when Thomas's face didn't soften, when the hard stare persisted and his expression didn't waver, Daniel turned white. He left the room shaking. Ann immediately followed him out, swearing at Thomas as she went. Thomas could hear his son sobbing next door, Ann attempting to comfort him, but he couldn't bring himself to walk through to them.

Later that night Thomas did apologise. He told Daniel he was tired from the long drive and all that had happened. He put his arms around his son's thin shoulders, which Daniel allowed whilst remaining stiff and unyielding. Was this something else broken? Thomas wondered.

Ann and the children ate sandwiches quietly whilst Thomas checked all the windows were closed and double-checked the front door was locked. It was, but he wasn't happy with how it rattled in its frame, it seemed flimsy to him, a good kick and it would give. He glanced around the hallway and spotted the chest of drawers underneath the coat rack. He heaved it to the door. It was heavy and a good fit. The door secure, Thomas realised he had to be in bed. Without saying goodnight to Ann or the children he went to the bedroom and dropped onto the ancient, rolling mattress. He wished he'd brought something to drink, anything to knock him out, to stop him thinking, to stop him from being with himself.

The next morning the family was as quiet as the night before. The children had realised that this wasn't a usual family holiday and had already asked Ann how long they would be staying for. Harriet, the child who never moaned, who never caused a fuss, said, quietly but firmly, that she wanted to go home. Ann tried to kick-start things and rallied the children into the car and drove to the nearest town or village she could find to buy food for the days ahead. She allowed the children to choose a selection of sweets and chocolate each, everything they wanted, all rules out of the window.

Thomas took the opportunity to walk around the cottage and see where they were in daylight. The travel agent only had a summary of the house's facilities, he'd not seen a photograph, and it was not what he'd expected. He'd imagined a thick-stoned squat little place, perhaps with a stone-floored hallway, white walls and beams across low ceilings and an open fire. But this was a bungalow which could have been plucked from any estate in England and dropped next to the quiet road in wild, remote northern Britain. It was nobody's idea of a rural cottage, but that didn't matter. It was about the location. The hundreds of miles they were away from Abbeystead and their own beautiful house. It wasn't working though. Thomas felt his hands begin to shake. Panic rose in him and threatened to overwhelm. He needed to escape somehow. But when you've already run to the north of the country above your own, when there is only empty land and then miles of sea, where is there left to run to? Thomas looked around. Behind the house was a field and then a steep hill. He thought if he walked to the top of the hill he might feel better, calmer. Up there he would be able to see for miles. He walked for thirty minutes, his hands resting on his thighs, his breathing heavy and hard. He reached the top, sweating and tired. He looked around him. Everything here was bigger. Wider. The Highlands made Abbeystead seem model-like and quaint in comparison. Here Thomas wasn't even a pinprick on the landscape. Below him he saw their car approach the bungalow and stop. The children stood at the open boot whilst Ann passed out bags and then they all walked to the front door. What a thing to see: his wife and children, walking together. Thomas's legs went. He sank to his haunches and dropped into the heather. He was inconsolable.

Twenty

There was loud banging on Raymond's door. He turned in his bed and looked at the clock; it was seven in the morning. Those girls from next door are back, he thought, even with a dead dad they want to cause trouble. But then he realised it was far too early for them, so he crept over to his window and peered down. A policeman and policewoman stood there.

They drove him to Pursely, twenty miles away, without saying a word to him, speaking only small talk to each other. At the station they led him to a room at the back of the building and then, after a few minutes, a man who introduced himself as Inspector Harrison appeared.

Raymond had given the police a statement, along with Thomas and Ann, on the day Keith Sullivan had turned up shouting he had a knife. He'd told the police, and the Nortons, that the man had been his neighbour in Etherton. 'Sorry,' he kept saying to

Thomas, 'I didn't have a clue.' But he felt complicit in it all so he knew what was coming from the inspector in front of him.

The room was hot and airless and Raymond was already sweating before the interview began.

'Relax, Mr Farren,' Harrison said. 'Can we get you a drink of water?'

Raymond shook his head. He didn't want to slow the process down. The men looked at each other for a moment. Harrison's head was shaped like a peanut, his skin was smooth and tanned, scattered with brown freckles, his hair was short and blond. He was wearing a pink shirt and a silver tie and a black pointy shoe poked out from underneath the side of the table. He looked to Raymond like a man who would never speak to him in a hundred years, unless it was his job to do so now, in this room.

'I'm looking at the statement you gave us earlier, Mr Farren. The day Keith Sullivan threatened the Nortons with a knife.'

He looked to Raymond as if for confirmation and Raymond nodded.

'You are Raymond Farren. You own a house, eleven Granville Road, where you sometimes stay, but more often you stay in a caravan on a farm where you work, in Abbeystead.'

'I used to,' Raymond said. 'That job isn't mine any more.'

Harrison made a note.

'You are friends with Thomas Norton, who also lives in Abbeystead.'

'Yes,' Raymond said.

'And your neighbour, in Etherton, was Keith Sullivan.'

'I know.'

'The man we suspect was part of a team of men who held the Nortons hostage, robbed the bank and then later returned alone and threatened the family with a knife.'

'Yes.'

'How did you become friends with Thomas Norton?'

'I was walking one night when a car was set alight close to his house. There was an explosion and I went to see what had happened and he was already there.'

'And you became friends after that?'

'Yes.'

'So you knew about his job. You knew where he worked?'

'We spoke about our jobs, yes.'

'You say you were walking. They live in a remote spot, several miles from where you worked and stayed. Why were you so close to their house?'

'It was night. I don't always sleep well so I walk in the forest at night.'

'So you know Bleasdale Forest well? You know your way through the trees?'

'Yes,' Raymond said. 'Very well,' he added, keen to tell the absolute truth.

'And how well did you know Keith Sullivan?'

'I didn't really know him. I knew who he was but that was all.'

'You never spoke to him? The man who lived next door to a house you own?'

'He spoke to me a few times. He was hard to avoid.'

'So you did know him a little?'

'Just in passing. I tried to avoid him.'

'Why would you try and avoid your neighbour?'

'I didn't like him.'

'Why?'

'He didn't seem to like me. And he was, I don't know. I could hear him shouting through the wall when he was drunk. And his daughters used to turn the bins over in my yard, spread the rubbish around, and ring my phone all the time, shout things about me. I tried to avoid all of them.'

'Did you report this trouble?'

Raymond shook his head.

'Why not?'

'My life wasn't there. My life was in Abbeystead, Bleasdale. I just wanted to be away from there.'

Harrison flattened his tie against his shirt.

'What we aren't saying, Mr Farren, is that you knew the man who held the Nortons hostage and robbed a bank. And you knew the Nortons. And these people lived almost twenty miles away from each other.'

'I know,' said Raymond.

'You know what?'

'What you said . . .'

'It's some coincidence, is it not?'

Raymond shook his head.

'It's not a coincidence?'

'No. It is a coincidence.'

Harrison shifted in his chair. 'You say you never spoke to Keith Sullivan about Thomas Norton. You never mentioned his job, where he lived?'

'Never. Not a word.'

'How are you doing for money, Mr Farren?'

'I don't have much. Hardly any. I got paid for working on the farm, but not a lot. And that's ended now. I've managed to save a little to live off until I find something else. But I don't spend much.'

'What about the house in Etherton? How do you pay for that?'

'My mother left me it. It's paid for.'

'And you get by?'

'Just about. My meals were included at the farm and there were no bills living in the caravan. Because I wasn't at the house all the time the bills from there were small too.'

'And at no point were you aware of Mr Sullivan's plans?'

'No.'

'And, to confirm, at no point you told Mr Sullivan about Thomas Norton, his job and where he lived?'

'No.'

Harrison picked up the papers in front of him and stood up abruptly.

'OK. Thank you, Mr Farren.'

Back in Etherton Raymond sat in his chair in the front room, but he couldn't settle. He pulled his bike from under the stairs and set off for Abbeystead. He'd been finding the ride harder lately, the hills steeper and longer, and halfway up Marshaw Fell he was suddenly struggling for breath. He climbed off his bike and rested his hands on his knees, gasping. He thought he might be dying for a second and then he told himself, 'It's just stress, it's just stress,' and slowly his breathing came back to him. He arrived at the Nortons' shaky and exhausted.

They had been back from Scotland for three days. Thomas was at work, the children were at school, but Ann was home and invited Raymond in. She filled a glass of water for him and told him to sit down. His hand shook as he lifted the glass to his mouth and it took him a while before he could tell Ann what had happened that morning. Ann calmed him as much as she could, but Raymond became more agitated and upset.

'You don't think that I knew about it all, do you? Does Thomas think that?'

'Don't be silly, Raymond, nobody thought that.'

'But they were asking if I'd told Sullivan about Thomas's job. They were saying I was the connection.' Raymond looked at Ann. 'I didn't say anything,' he said. 'I didn't say a word to him about you.'

'We believe you, Raymond,' Ann said. 'We never thought anything else for a second.'

'But after the robbery, I didn't see Thomas for weeks, months,' Raymond said.

'He didn't see anyone! He barely saw me or the

children. He's been depressed, Raymond, it had nothing to do with you. And we didn't even know Keith Sullivan was one of the men until he came back that day, Raymond. You're working yourself up for no reason.'

'But he was my neighbour. All along, he was just next door.'

Raymond stood up and began pacing the kitchen. There were deep lines on his forehead, his cheeks were red and there was nothing Ann could say to calm him down. She went to the hallway and called Thomas.

Thomas arrived half an hour later. He rushed into the house. 'What is it?' he said, looking around the room. 'What's the matter?' he asked Raymond.

'Calm down, Thomas,' Ann said.

Raymond looked to Ann.

'The police have been speaking to him. Because his house in Etherton is next door to Sullivan's. They've been asking him questions, saying he must have known things.'

Thomas looked at Raymond.

'Did you?' he asked.

'Thomas . . .' Ann said, in a low voice.

'It's a fair question, isn't it? How else did a man

who lived fifteen miles away know where I lived and what job I did?'

Raymond's big head dropped. He closed his eyes and shook his head.

'Think about it,' Thomas said. 'It's not an unreasonable question to ask him. Is it? And he knew his job at the farm was ending, he knew he would be needing money.'

'He chased him, Thomas! While you stood there he chased the little bastard!'

'Maybe that was all part of it.'

'I think you better leave,' Ann said.

Raymond stood up.

'Not you, Raymond. This man here.' She was pointing at Thomas.

Twenty-One

Thomas sat on the thin bed at Redgate Guest House. He'd driven around for a couple of hours before ending up there, but he knew it would be his destination as soon as he thought of the place; there wasn't anywhere else he could think to go. He'd never been a man with many friends but it struck him as he drove the empty country roads wondering where to take himself, how he'd let the friendships he'd enjoyed over the years slip away.

The woman who gave him the room was the same woman as eight years before, just heavier now and with shorter hair, but if she recognised Thomas she gave no indication. She handed him his key and pointed him on his way. He remembered the room from his previous stays. A dark red carpet, a cheap pine wardrobe and chest of drawers, thin cream curtains patterned with red flowers and a small bed against the wall. A print of three glossy purple mountains hung in a silver frame on the wall.

A memory came to him and he went to check. He pulled open the wardrobe door and looked at the left-hand side of the interior wall. It was as he remembered, a list of names of men, and some women, who'd stayed in the room ran down the inside panel. The list was a lot longer than it had been; it was on its third column now. He spotted his hand, about fifteen names down, TRN, just his initials, as some others had chosen to do. Thomas Richard Norton. He noticed the pencil, resting on a ledge, but he didn't pick it up. He didn't want this stay recorded, even in pencil on the inside of a wardrobe.

The first night Thomas ate in a local pub and drank a few drinks. He thought about Ann and the children back at the house, he wondered what they were all doing. After Raymond left Thomas had tried to reason with Ann. He apologised for accusing Raymond, he apologised for Scotland, for how he'd been behaving.

'But don't you see,' he'd said, desperately. 'All this worry is for us. For you and the children, for all of us.'

Ann looked at him and shook her head. 'It doesn't feel like that, Thomas. Please go. For a few days, for however long, but please leave.' She pulled a suitcase out from the wardrobe and threw it on the bed.

'What about the children?' Thomas asked.

'I'll speak to them. They'll be fine,' Ann said. 'They're tougher than you think.'

'You really want me to go?' he asked, half an hour later in the front room, suitcase in his hand.

'I need you to go, Thomas. Living with you, it's exhausting. I want you to get better; I'll help you get better, but right now,' Ann started to cry, 'please give me some time without you.'

Thomas put down the suitcase and stepped forward but Ann tensed at his approach and held up her hand. 'No,' she said, through her tears, so he turned and left.

In the guesthouse Thomas flicked through the channels but nothing held his attention so he turned the television off and pulled a straight-backed chair away from the wall and placed it in the middle of the room. He sat and tried to remember how this was supposed to be done. He lowered his hands to his knees, closed his eyes, breathed in through his nose and exhaled slowly. He tried to calm his thoughts and focus on the breath in his nostrils, on the rise and fall of his belly. He counted one on the in-breath, one on the out-breath and then two and two up until he reached ten, when he started again. 'Don't become frustrated when your mind wanders,' Dr Barbour had told him. 'It's natural. Just acknowledge that you were thinking, or worrying, or planning and then bring the mind back to the breath.'

Dr Barbour was right, Thomas quickly realised. The mind did like to wander. He saw Ann, crying in her chair, shaking her head at him. He thought of the children, in bed by now, and wondered what Ann had told them, how they'd reacted. It was a few seconds before he realised he wasn't following his breath. 'Thinking, thinking,' he thought, and attempted to lasso his chasing mind and haul it back.

Thomas persevered for ten minutes. Ten minutes of trying to stem anxious, skittering thoughts and failing miserably. He felt uncomfortable in the stiff chair, his back was beginning to ache and his stomach was full from the beer and the meal he'd eaten earlier. But more than that, the attempt at relaxing, at silencing his thoughts, only made him more agitated. He could feel the tension inside him increase. When the thudding from the next room began, in tandem with thin, breathy yelps, he put the chair back against the wall and turned the television on.

He'd taken enough clothes from the house to get him through the week but hadn't thought of the weekend so found himself standing outside Raymond's house in his work suit on Saturday morning at half past nine.

The door opened slowly, Raymond peering through the gap suspiciously until he saw it was Thomas and opened the door fully.

'Can I come in?' Thomas asked and Raymond stepped to one side.

They sat in two chairs in the front room with the peeling wallpaper curling around them.

'I'm sorry, Raymond,' Thomas said. 'There isn't much more to it than that. I'm sorry.'

'I didn't say a word to him,' Raymond said. 'Not a word.'

'I know. I was exhausted and I lashed out.'

'It's alright,' Raymond said.

'Well, it isn't. But I do mean it, I am sorry. I found myself saying the words and I couldn't stop them.'

They sat there in the cold, musty room in silence for a while.

'It was lashing out, Raymond,' Thomas said again. 'It was stupid of me.'

'All along he was living just there.' Raymond pointed at the wall to his left. 'I heard the man when he coughed.'

Both men looked at the flaky wall.

'Have the police had you back in?' Thomas asked.

Raymond shook his head. 'But if the phone rings I think it will be them. I thought that knock at the door was them again.'

'I'll talk to them,' Thomas said.

Raymond thanked him and they carried on sitting there.

They had lunch in a pub and then Thomas drove them to Abbeystead. He parked a couple of miles from his house and they walked through the trees.

They ended up at the road by Thomas's house. They stopped and looked at the place.

'Are you going in?' Raymond asked.

'I'm going to knock,' Thomas said. 'See where that gets me.'

Twenty-Two

Ann decided she still wanted a party. It was two weeks after Thomas's birthday, a week after his brief stay at the guesthouse, but she was determined. He was trying his best, she could see that. He didn't say anything about the monitor she'd unplugged from his office and stashed at the back of their wardrobe. He didn't ask for his notebooks, filled with times, car registrations, makes and models, which were sat firmly underneath the monitor. And she noted that he wasn't getting up as early in the morning and creeping through the trees on the other side of the road, checking his traps. In fact, for him, he was sleeping quite late.

'It's these pills,' he said one morning, a few days after he'd moved back in, looking bleary and ruffled at the kitchen table. 'Dr Barbour said some people have trouble sleeping on them, but I seem to be the opposite. They knock me out. And some of the dreams . . .'

'You've started taking pills?' Ann asked.

'Well, the meditation didn't seem to work for me.'

'You were meditating? Jesus, Thomas, why don't you tell me anything?'

'I only tried it a few times, at the guesthouse. And I'm telling you about the pills now.'

Ann sighed. 'And? So? How are they working out?'

'My teeth feel funny. Tired and weird dreams.'

'But in other areas?'

'Too soon to say. I will need to be on them for a few weeks before we know if they make a difference.'

'Thank you for trying them, Thomas.'

'Well, it doesn't have to be forever. Dr Barbour said to stick with them for a few months and then we can look at how I'm doing. Maybe lower the dose, take it from there.'

'And maybe cut back on the whisky too,' Ann said.

'No choice there.'

Ann smiled at him. She'd poured all the drink in the house down the sink.

She bought the food again, put the banners back up and finally tied the balloons to the front door. Thomas collected Raymond, Daniel was persuaded from his room and Harriet put on her favourite dress.

It was early evening and they were all sat around

the table. They'd eaten, sung happy birthday, Thomas had cut the cake and now they were all eating a slice. Everyone had been quiet for a while when Daniel, with a purple party hat resting awkwardly on his head, the elastic cutting into his bony chin, looked around the table and said, 'This isn't even a proper party. This is just us wearing stupid hats and eating cake.'

It didn't strike Thomas as immediately funny. But then he looked around the table from person to person and it hit him. His laughter started slowly, a few splutters at first, but then it took hold and shook him. He had to spit his drink back into his glass because he couldn't swallow. His laughter came out in high, uncontrolled squeaks, his chest rising and falling like he'd run a race.

'I'm sorry,' he kept saying, holding his hands up. 'I'm sorry.'

Just when he thought he couldn't laugh any more, when it would hurt to laugh more, Raymond, his own green party hat resting like a pea on top of his large head, turned to Ann and said, 'Well, it's the best party I've ever been to.'

At that, Thomas was gone. He shook uncontrollably. He laid his head on the table, stretched out his arms and wept with laughter.

'I'm sorry, I'm sorry,' he kept saying. 'It's a good party, it is. I'm sorry, I can't stop.' He laughed until he was weak in every bone in his body.

That night, with the children in bed, when Thomas had dropped Raymond back in Etherton, Ann and Thomas sat in the front room. Ann's record played behind them.

'Who is this?' Thomas asked.

'The Blue Nile,' Ann said.

'I like it,' Thomas said. 'I like his voice.'

'It always makes me think of you,' Ann said.

Thomas looked at Ann, with her feet underneath her, curled up in the chair and said, 'Really, why?'

'Once, not long after we'd moved here, we were driving home one night and it was playing on the radio and neither of us said anything. The song made me so happy, so excited about life. My heart felt full. We were driving through the trees, it was a summer night and warm and you were driving quite fast and it was the perfect music for the night. When it finished you said, "I love that song." I didn't know you'd even been listening properly and I didn't think it would be the type of song you would like.'

Thomas shook his head. 'I don't remember.'

'That's why I bought the album.'

Ann looked at Thomas and said, 'Do you remember? The last few weeks in Maltham?'

Thomas threw his head back against the sofa and looked at the ceiling. 'It was hectic. Trying to get the builders to finish this place, trying to be competent at work, and Harriet.'

'But the last few weeks, Thomas?'

Thomas closed his eyes, his face still raised to the ceiling. 'Harriet?' he asked.

'Yes, she was sleeping better. There would still be bad nights, but she was sleeping better, wasn't she?'

'That's how I remember it, yes,' Thomas said.

'Neither of us said anything.'

'What would be the point? We'd sold the house. We'd built this house. From a shell, from nothing. There was no halting what we'd started.'

'Do you think we did the right thing moving here, Thomas?'

'Remember though, at the time it seemed like the only thing we could do.'

'Do you miss Maltham? Do you miss the old house?'

Thomas opened his eyes. 'I didn't. For years I didn't. And now, I don't know if I'm missing the house, or just a time before when I wasn't as anxious, as screwed up. A time when you were happier.'

'I'm not unhappy,' Ann said.

'That's hardly a glowing endorsement, is it?'

'It's enough. I think it's quite a thing to achieve – the absence of pain.'

Ann looked at Thomas, with his eyes closed tightly again, his head tipped back, his hands held stiffly together in his lap. He looked tight, explosive. He looked exhausted. 'The absence of pain,' he said, and laughed.

'I still love you, Thomas,' Ann said.

'Thank you,' Thomas said. A tear rolled down his cheek and Ann went to sit with him.

Twenty-Three

The young men arrived in a van at eight on a Monday morning and set to with sledgehammers. Raymond hated it. Strangers in his house, and the state of it – what would they think of him? And the way they went for the walls – young pimply lads, all bone and shaved heads, as skinny as the handles of the massive hammers they swung unsteadily above their heads.

'Excuse me,' the youngest-looking one said, after they'd been there ten minutes.

'Are there shops near by?'

'What do you want to buy?' Raymond asked.

The lad shrugged and said, 'Sweets.'

They're children! Raymond thought. Children are smashing up my house. The boy, informed where he could buy his sweets, happily swung the hammer into the wall with a thud. Plaster fell away, the bricks underneath cracked and the house shook with the trauma of it. Worried that his feeble house would collapse, and hating the noise and mess, Raymond left them to it and walked the streets of the town as slowly as he could, returning home at five to find bare bricks throughout the downstairs, sacks of wall-paper and plaster piled up in the front room, dust hanging in the air and covering everything in a thick, gritty layer. The house shocked and silent in the aftermath of it all. By the end of the second day a damp course had been injected into each of the walls and blue plastic sheets pinned to the bricks. Raymond had to give them credit – they knew how to work. And before he left the next morning he saw how the oldest lad marshalled the other three into action, hurried them along, set them jobs and made sure they knew what they were doing. The plastic sheets were boarded over and plastered, all of the work finished in three days.

Raymond enjoyed two quiet days before another van arrived. This time it was the central heating man, who unloaded a boiler, radiators and lengths of copper pipe. 'Copper, Mr Farren, I only use copper. The younger fitters would lay plastic, but I'm a copper man.' Raymond nodded, copper sounded better than plastic. It was easier with just one man working in the house, but Raymond still preferred to be out of the way whilst the work was being done. He didn't want to chat over a brew, to monitor the progress, to discuss the problems found and conquered along the way. After four days Raymond was presented with a safety certificate and an instruction booklet, and given a lesson on setting the boiler. Then the man tidied away his tools and left Raymond alone. It wasn't a cold night but Raymond fired up the boiler and let the heating run on full for three hours. He sat in his chair, all the windows closed, sweating like he was laying a fence in Abbeystead on the hottest day in August. As the sweat soaked into his shirt he imagined the house drying out, the damp air retreating, the air becoming clean and hard. And within days the house did smell differently, the sweet smell of dampness had begun to fade.

The day after the heating was installed Raymond set to work. He pulled the remaining wallpaper down from the walls, it fell away in clumps in most places, and he hacked and chiselled where it clung stubbornly. When each room was stripped Raymond called the plasterer in. Out of all the work that was done to the house, this was the least stressful for Raymond. And although it was messy, it was quiet, and after the banging, tearing and pulling, Raymond could finally see the house becoming new. He even stayed at home on the final afternoon and watched the plasterer turn messy, broken walls into smooth, flat surfaces. With all the plaster on the walls the house was back to being wet and cold, but each day Raymond could see the damp, dark patches shrinking and the plaster turning pink and hardening. He cranked up the heating to help it on its way and walked around the house touching the flat walls. Finally he bought the paint. Cheap emulsion for the undercoats, an expensive white emulsion to finish with. 'Don't skimp on the top coat,' the plasterer told him. 'It's not worth it, cheap paint will ruin the job.' It took Raymond a week to paint every room in the house, two undercoats and one final coat. He painted slowly and with precision, enjoying the work, the rhythm and reliability of it. He was sad when he painted his last stroke. Thomas had offered to help with the painting, but Raymond had thanked him and refused the offer. He could never say how grateful he was to Thomas and Ann for the loan they'd insisted on, even when Raymond told them he wasn't sure when he would ever earn the money to pay them back, but he wanted to work alone. And then, the brushes and rollers rinsed, the empty paint cans stacked in the backyard, the walls dry, it was finally done. Raymond couldn't quite believe it, but all around him were smooth white walls.

Twenty-Four

On Saturday morning Thomas and Ann dropped the children off with Ann's parents and visited three estate agents in Maltham. They managed to arrange three viewings for that day. The first house was too close to a main road, the second needed too much work doing, but the third house was beautiful. A detached house with gardens at the front and rear, nestled back from a quiet, tree-lined street. From the front bedroom you could see down onto the River Wyresdale and over to Beacon Fell. 'It's still like being in the countryside really,' Thomas said, as they stared out of the bedroom window, 'but it would be easier for town and there might be more children for Daniel and Harriet to play with.'

'Is this what you want, Thomas?' Ann asked. 'To move back to town?'

He shook his head. He didn't know, was the truth. 'What about you?' he asked.

'Well, there are things I would like about it. It

would be nice to be able to walk into town, to visit friends easily, not have to drive everywhere. But I would miss our house.'

'Would you?'

'I think I might even miss the trees.'

'I thought you hated the place.'

'I did, for a while.'

'I hated it too,' Thomas said. 'After that night anyway.'

Ann looked around the bedroom and back out to the river. 'This place is lovely.'

Thomas agreed that it was.

'But it's not what I want.'

'Why not?'

'Too many street lights, too much light pollution.'

*

Thomas was woken by the high warning beep of a reversing truck. It was seven in the morning. He pulled on a pair of trousers and a shirt and rushed downstairs. He found Ann, already dressed, talking to the truck driver, pointing to their back garden. On the back of the truck, tied down, were large wooden panels and a flat roof of some sort.

Ann turned to Thomas. 'I ordered it when you were staying at the guesthouse.'

'I was only gone a few days,' Thomas said.

'I know. I get a lot done when you're not hanging around getting in the way.'

All day there was crashing and sawing and drilling coming from the back garden. At four o'clock the men were done and called for Ann. She went to check that everything was as it should be. She came out of the building with her arms folded and a large grin on her face. She thanked the men and they packed up and left.

It was a large shed with a sliding roof. 'A sky shed,' Ann told Thomas. 'But it's more than a shed. Because the telescope will be in the shed all the time, in all weathers, they fit waterproof sheeting to the walls and then they clad them, and look inside.'

Thomas walked into the sky shed and looked around. There was space inside for a desk and a bed even. Ann saw Thomas's eyes widen. 'No,' she said, and pushed him to the door.

Twenty-Five

It was Saturday night. The next morning Thomas was coming and Raymond would show him the house, the transformation, before they drove back to Abbeystead, to walk a new hill or a favourite route. As the sun set on Etherton every road, side street and backyard turned darker and smaller in the dusk. Cats woke on beds, yawned, stretched and padded downstairs, ready for a shift patrolling the alleys. Landlords turned on lights to outdoor signs, made sure drinks cabinets were stacked and barrels ready. Men sucked in their paunches and pulled their best jeans on. Women did their make-up, angling their heads, fishfacing into mirrors. Older children were given the run of the television and left in charge of younger children. Pizzas were pushed into ovens. The streets and pubs began to fill. Raymond sat in his front room, staring at the wall. He could stare at his new walls for hours. They'd burnt his caravan in the end, he'd heard, it had been the cheapest thing to do. But he didn't care. In the smooth white wall in front of him Raymond saw fields and forests. He saw the hanging hawk and the hunted rabbit, the stream in high field, frozen with ice, the shippen, glowing on a drowsy summer night. In the front room of 11 Granville Road, with his arms at his side, sitting with the qualities of a mountain, Raymond was with it all.

Twenty-Six

Harriet lay in bed, her duvet pulled up to her chin, wide awake. The trees had been groaning and shaking for nearly an hour and now they roared as the storm moved across the valley and into the forest. A block of light fell into her room and her mum stood in the open doorway.

'Are you OK, love?' she asked. 'I think it's going to get noisy soon.'

'I'm OK, Mum,' Harriet said.

'Not scared?'

Harriet shook her head.

'Well, come and find me if it gets worse.'

The room turned dark again as the door closed but filled with light seconds later when lightning struck. Two more strikes and then thunder – the loudest noise Harriet had ever heard, an explosion of sound, a deep heavy bombing.

Daniel appeared in front of her.

'Are you scared?' he asked. His eyes wide.

'A bit,' she lied.

He clambered on her bed and sat with his back to the wall.

'I'll stay then,' he said.

More lightning, more thunder, the trees howling through it all.

Ann returned. She sat on the bed too and they all stared at the curtained window as if it was a cinema screen.

'The trees sound like they are screaming,' Harriet said.

The storm was driven by its own energy, it grew stronger, the winds wilder, the rain harder. Harriet wondered if it would ever end or if this would be how it was now. Was this the new world? She'd almost reconciled herself to the idea of an eternal storm when, slowly, the winds began to ease. A few gusts returned but the battle had been lost, the heart gone. Thunder only muttered now, disconsolate in retreat. And then silence for a moment before rain began to fall quietly. Daniel left as quickly as he'd appeared, Ann kissed Harriet on her forehead and tucked her in tightly, her door was closed and she was alone.

Harriet freed herself from the bed and walked to the window, pulled back the curtains and looked out to the trees. They were battered and wild, ripped at and exhausted. She thought of her dad carrying her through those trees as a baby in the black of the night and a chill ran through her. She shivered and smiled. She heard her mum leave the bathroom, cross the landing and close the bedroom door. Her dad snored loudly. Harriet raised her hands to close the curtains but stopped, she would leave them open. She crossed the room, climbed into bed and slept.

Acknowledgements

Thank you:
Kate, Antony Harwood, Kate Murray-Browne, Julian Loose and everyone at Faber.